Once Upon A Midnight Dream

Chronicles of the Westbrook Brides

BOOK 10

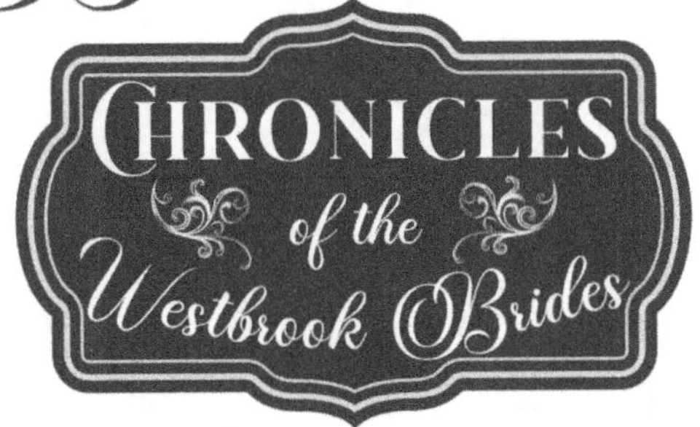

USA Today Bestselling Author

Collette Cameron®

SWEET-TO-SPICY TIMELESS ROMANCE®

Blue Rose Romance® LLC

collette@collettecameronbooks.com
collettecameron.com
eBook ISBN: 978-1-955259-57-6
Print Book ISBN: 978-1-966087-00-7

PRAISE FOR...ONCE UPON A MIDNIGHT DREAM

COLLETTE CAMERON®

See What Readers Are Saying About
Once Upon a Midnight Dream!

★★★★★ "What a deliciously different storyline for the ending of a wonderful series." ~ *Pat Robinson*

★★★★★ "This is a sweet and wonderful story. The author uses a simple and smooth cadence for the dialogue and narrative throughout the story. It keeps the reader invested in the characters and their lives. This is a wonderful story to start the new year with." ~ *Suzette*

★★★★★ "The storyline was very entertaining, and there were a lot of interesting secondary characters, humorous moments, and some sweet romantic scenes." ~ *Marilyn*

★★★★★ "This beautiful Novella will entice you from start to finish and is a must read. Highly recommend." ~ *Yamlan*

★★★★★ "I thoroughly enjoyed this engaging story. I loved the characters of Lilly and Leyton/Zander. The epilogue brings a satisfying end to this series. I just love Colette's style of writing, it's just so easy to read, always with a touch of humour and a happy ending." ~ *Cheryl*

"Zander, why are you looking at me like that?

"Because, my darling, I desperately want to kiss you."

"Oh.
"You do?"

"Very, very, much."

ONCE UPON A MIDNIGHT DREAM

CHRONICLES OF THE WESTBROOK BRIDES
BOOK TEN

COLLETTE CAMERON®

FREE BOOK!

JOIN MY EXCLUSIVE MAILING LIST
Collette Cameron Newsletter

AND GET A FREE EBOOK!

https://bit.ly/TheRegencyRoseGift

Plus Sneak Peeks, Giveaways, Contests, Exclusive Content, and More... P.S. I promise only good stuff ~ **no** spam!

DEDICATION

For precious baby R.

Gigi loves you.

PROLOGUE

The outskirts of the sleepy village of Prudhoe, England

Late August 1828—almost midnight

Breath coming in heaving gasps and holding one bruised arm across his throbbing ribs, Captain Layton Westbrook grasped the fencepost with his badly lacerated free hand.

Cursing and grimacing against the lancing pain, he dragged his foot onto the wooden fence's lowest rail. The effort cost him mightily, and a wave of dizziness threatened to send him to his knees.

Again.

Nearby, an owl's haunting hoot rent the air.

Almost immediately, the sounds of a not-so-small animal thrashing about in the hedgerow slightly behind and to Layton's left muted the booming call. Heaven help him should the creature be a female badger returning to her burrow and cubs.

Motionless and holding his breath, Layton strained his ears until the scurrying and crackling in the underbrush abated. Only then did he dare raise his sweaty, blood-caked face and draw in a handful of shallow breaths.

Steady on, old chap.

You have been in worse scrapes.

Though an officer in the army for two decades, except for the explosion that blinded him in one eye, Layton had not. He shoved the memories of that trauma to the back of his mind. This was not the time to reflect on his dead wife's perfidy.

Right now, concentrating on surviving and evading capture must be his sole focus.

And, of course, getting word to his family that he was alive, if not particularly hale and hearty.

Not a single doubt beset him that the Earl of Highbury's henchmen still pursued him. The earl could not afford for Layton to escape and tell the world what the blackguard had done.

What Layton did not know, however, was how quickly his abductors had discovered his absence and followed him. Or, if they had been fooled by the false trail to Henshaw he had laid, delaying his flight by several precious minutes.

He prayed his ruse had worked.

Not that he deserved God's grace, but mayhap the good Lord had deigned to show him favor, just this once.

The thin silvery crescent suspended in the heavens did little to illuminate the night, but at least no clouds blurred the millions of sparkling stars.

Darkness did not bother him.

In fact, he usually found it soothing and peaceful.

This was *not* one of those times.

As a captain in His Majesty's Army, Layton had engaged in stealthy nocturnal assignments in blackness darker than the

Earl of Hell's waistcoat and as dangerous as encountering the devil himself.

Compared to those life-threatening adventures, tonight was simply a jaunt to Vauxhall or Covent Garden.

Or so he kept repeating to himself as he had slogged onward toward Hexham.

It was a colossal lie, of course.

No one had ever held him prisoner or tortured him before.

An enormous shadow passed overhead; its great wings outstretched.

The eagle-owl he had heard calling earlier.

With considerable effort, Layton levered his other foot onto the low rail.

A ragged groan tore from his throat as pain radiated throughout his body with the movement.

Besides more than one broken rib, fingers, knuckles, multiple lacerations, and a fractured nose, his foggy brain, blurry vision, and the crushing pain in his head suggested he had sustained a concussion too.

Not before he had given as good as he'd received, by God. If his mouth was not so bloody and battered, his lips chapped and scabbed, he might have summoned a triumphant grin.

His throat dry as ash, he swallowed.

Devil it, he was deuced thirsty.

A fulminating wave of weakness and dizziness cascaded over him.

I cannot do it.

I cannot go on.

Fighting faintness, which could prove deadly should he succumb, he lowered his forehead to the highest rail and, resting his head there, sucked in shallow rasps of cool air.

You must, Layton Alexander Vale Westbrook.

Cassius's and Beatrice's lives might well depend on it.

Other Westbrooks' lives too.

But the truth was, Layton had already failed Cassius.

Pain scoured him.

A dagger impaling his heart could not have hurt worse.

He had promised his youngest brother that he would return for him and Beatrice after leaving them in the forest glen to seek help at Hefferwickshire House—their familial home and the duchy's grand country estate.

That had been two—no—three days ago.

He scrunched his forehead.

Or had it been four?

Layton honestly did not know.

Everything had become a blur.

With his mind befuddled from the beatings he had endured, as well as lack of food and water, he could not recall the passage of time with any certainty.

One thing he did know, however, beyond any doubt.

The peer responsible for his abduction had no qualms about killing anyone who stood in his way, including the Earl of Highbury's niece, Beatrice Fairfax.

Not in the habit of praying, Layton sent up a silent plea for divine intervention, nevertheless.

God, help me.

Please let Cassius and Beatrice be safe.

Four tries and as many tumbles later, amidst a bevy of curses that would have caused a seasoned sailor to blush crimson, he finally flopped onto his back in the foggy meadow on the other side.

Staring at the twinkling stars in the jet-black sky, Layton fought to remain conscious, each breath lancing him with burning pain.

The chilly ground permeated his clothing, and a shiver shook him.

Wounded and utterly spent, he could not continue much farther.

How much distance had he put between himself and the men the mad-as-a-hatter, Earl of Highbury, had hired to abduct him?

Layton guessed he had traveled three, mayhap, four miles.

Not bloody far enough to be safe.

A horse would have been most welcome, but there had been no sign of his gray bay gelding. Likely, the animal had been sold. Besides, Layton was not positive he could have saddled or mounted a horse.

Even with his arms wrapped around his torso for support, his broken ribs made running impossible. He could only manage a rapid, faltering walk. He hoped anyone glimpsing him through the vapor rising from the meadow would have mistaken him for a drunken tippler, stumbling his way home.

Eyes squeezed shut and grinding his teeth together against the agony coursing through every pore in his body, Layton rolled over, pushed to his knees, and then used the sturdy fence to pull himself upright.

More rustling sounded from the hedgerow, and a chorus of field crickets chirping to attract mates filled the air.

Sagging against the structure, he squinted at the misty meadow.

Just a little farther.

Enough to ensure he had eluded his captors.

Before dawn's glow lit the sky, Layton hoped to find a place to rest and seek help in Hexham.

In the distance, several manor houses dotted the horizon, their grand chimneys lined up like proud, shadowy sentinels against the midnight sky. Surely amongst the residents, someone knew of his father, the powerful Duke of Latham.

One mention of his adopted father's name, and Layton was confident aid would be forthcoming swiftly. Especially if he hinted at a generous reward for discretion and speed.

Hunched over, a fresh trickle of blood oozing down his

forehead into his one good eye, Layton stumbled forward, forcing his legs into a clumsy trot. He had only traveled a few yards before he tripped over a grass-covered rock and crashed to the ground, striking his injured head.

Sweet Jesus.

Nausea swirled in his belly, and he released a ragged moan.

It was too much.

His mind and spirit were willing, but his broken body had forsaken him.

The burbling of a nearby brook soothed his tortured soul.

I am sorry, Cassius.

Blackness and despair enshrouded Layton as he sank into oblivion.

ONE

A cozy bedchamber in Kelston Hall Children's Home
On the outskirts of the Village of Prudhoe

Middle of September 1828—early morning

Lavender?

With the sluggishness of an opium addict, the man slowly roused from his slumber and twitched his nostrils, while allowing his eyes to remain shut. He ached in places he did not know could hurt.

Severe beatings tended to do that.

He furrowed his forehead.

I have been beaten.

Peculiar, he remembered being pummeled, but not who had thrashed him or where the pounding had occurred. For that matter, what he could recall about *anything* would scarcely fill a thimble.

His memory was as empty as his hollow stomach gnawing at his spine.

To still the panic rearing its gargoyle head at that horrific revelation, he focused on the familiar, comforting scent that had stirred him from sleep.

Yes, definitely lavender.

Still groggy, and with his eyes closed, he sniffed.

Hmm.

A slightly earthy scent also lingered, as did a pungent, medicinal aroma with a hint of sweetness and spice.

Poultices, salves, or tinctures?

To treat his injuries?

Bloody irregular.

What went on here?

Senses not yet fully attune, eyelids weighted closed, and limbs leaden, he inhaled deeply.

Other, lighter, more pleasing aromas teased his nose.

He sniffed again.

Lemon? Wildflowers? Sunshine?

Sunshine?

What the devil?

Have I gone mad?

Where the sodding blazes am I?

He vaguely recalled running, gasping for air—pain riddling his body and head—and finally collapsing in a meadow after escaping.

Wait...

An imprecise image flitted across his beleaguered mind and then floated away before he could grasp hold and bring it into full focus.

An impression remained, nonetheless.

Someone had abducted him.

But who?

Why?

Again, he could vaguely recall the event, but not the details surrounding the incident.

With considerable effort, he fought the cumbersome

cobwebs and wet wool besieging his mind, and mustering every ounce of determination he possessed, he groped his way to full wakefulness.

Wrinkling his nose again and drawing in a deep breath, while simultaneously creasing his forehead, he forced the millstones from his eyelids.

His senses told him dawn drew near.

They also screamed he was not alone.

Alarm throttled through his veins.

A soft sound beside his bed made him bolt upright, ready to defend himself once more.

An agonized gasp rushed past his dry lips as searing, molten fire speared his skull straight into his brain while scorching rapiers impaled his ribs.

Holy Mother of God!

Breath hissed from between clenched teeth as another groan ripped from his throat while he clutched his throbbing head, fighting to stay conscious.

He barely registered the bandages circling his head, ribs, and hands.

Nausea ripped through his stomach and throttled up his throat as a wave of excruciating pain threatened to cleave his head from his neck.

By God, he would welcome decapitation if it meant an end to the agony.

Desperate to tamp down the bile tapping against his teeth, he made a strangled noise in the back of his throat.

I am going to be sick.

In the dim pre-dawn light, a form in flowing white swiftly rose from beside his bed, sending a cloud of feminine fragrance wafting past his face.

Oh, God.

His tormented stomach could not stand anymore.

He gagged. Then gagged again.

"Oh, dear." She touched his shoulder, the pressure gentle and comforting. "You poor thing. I shall fetch a basin."

Even with the pain-induced haze assaulting him, he registered several details in the muted half-light.

Woman.

Average height.

English.

Middle to late thirties.

Educated speech.

A moment later, she produced a porcelain washbasin, and to his utter humiliation, he heaved his guts out as she held it before him. Not that there was much in his empty-as-a-miser's-charity-box stomach.

When he finally stopped retching, he collapsed back onto the pillows, mortified and weak.

The pale pinks, oranges, and purples peeking through the lace curtains announced dawn's imminent arrival.

"Queasiness is to be expected with a head wound, especially when one has a concussion." She spoke matter-of-factly, her tone low and modulated, kind but not patronizing. "It shall pass in time, although I know at present that is not much comfort to you."

Bloody right.

It is not.

The stranger turned from him and after placing the basin on a nearby commode, slipped on her wrapper, tying it at her waist. With practiced efficiency, she set about lighting a lamp.

Squinting, he blinked as the soft golden glow filled the unremarkable room, revealing the small chamber's door standing open.

Glancing downward, he registered the white nightshirt covering his torso.

I sleep nude.

The ruffled nightshirt was not his.

Not only did he sleep naked, but he would never wear anything with as much lace as this garment sported.

How could he recall that insignificant tidbit but nothing else?

One hand resting on the wrought iron, her head cocked slightly, the woman stood at the foot of the bed and studied him. Those intelligent dark brown eyes beneath winged brows several shades darker than her plaited hair probed him, pausing for a half-second on his damaged eye.

Ah, another morsel that he recalled.

He had lost vision in one eye.

Resisting the urge to touch his face to ensure the black leather patch hid the cloudy orb, he forced himself to take a mental inventory of his surroundings.

Already having concluded he wore another's rather hideous nightshirt—*what man in his right mind would choose to wear such a ridiculous thing?*—he noted the bandages artfully wrapped around his knuckles. He had also felt a dressing on his head when he'd clutched it earlier, and the vice-like pressure on his ribs suggested bindings encased his torso as well.

He lay in a narrow bed covered with a colorful quilt that appeared to have been constructed from a variety of fabrics with no apparent pattern. The other furniture comprised a straight-back chair upon which lay a once-green, rather flat, square velvet cushion, a small scuffed secretary, and the commode, upon which the plain white pitcher and basin sat.

Next to the bed, a small table acted as a nightstand. A wardrobe situated beside the door, along with two slightly crooked, dried-and-faded framed floral arrangements hanging on the same wall as the window, completed the simple décor.

Not stark, per se, but not opulent by any stretch of the imagination either.

A hazy vision of an elaborate black-and-white-tiled marble

entry skittered across his memory before evaporating as swiftly as a droplet of water upon a roaring fire.

He pointed his attention to the floor.

No rugs covered the clean, plain wood, but a pile of blankets and a pillow lay between his bed and the wall.

She slept there.

Why?

TWO

The same cozy bedchamber

After a few confusion-filled seconds had passed

With his one good eye, he studied her.

Her benign expression revealed nothing.

One thing was certain; he had never been so sodding feeble in his entire life. In truth, he doubted he could stand, let alone defend himself, should the need arise.

Wait...

He knew how to defend himself.

Another memory darted into his mind and was gone just as quickly.

A soldier—he was a soldier.

A slight smile formed on her mouth—a mouth Society would deem too full.

Another hint, that.

He knew something of High Society.

Not typical of an enlisted soldier.

An officer then?

Yes, that made sense.

He allowed himself the briefest glance over her voluptuous figure.

Le Beau Monde would consider her too plump as well.

He, however, thought she radiated health and a rare purity.

She smelled nice too.

"I am Lilibet Granger, the director and headmistress of this establishment, Kelston Hall Children's Home."

That explained the room's sparseness.

Orphanages were notoriously short of funds.

She brushed a strand of flaxen hair that had escaped the tight plaits on either side of her oval face. She was not pretty in the classical sense, but there was an aura of wholesomeness about her that appealed to him. Her velvety-brown eyes, framed by lush, sooty lashes, were her best features.

Unremarkable in its simplicity and modesty, her faded blue night robe did not quite hide her generous curves.

He felt certain she missed nothing in that cool, calm assessment of him.

"The children and I found you in the back meadow close to a fortnight ago."

A fortnight?

That long?

"Actually..." Another slight smile tipped her mouth upward at the corners.

She was almost pretty when she smiled.

"Our milk cows, Clover and Buttercup, found you first. Their distressed mooing caught our attention." She waved a long-fingered hand in the air. "Hence your presence here."

Her focus shifted to the window before she stepped away and parted the curtains, allowing him a glimpse of the glorious sunrise.

"You had no identification on you, so we could not

contact anyone on your behalf, though we did ask around Prudhoe," she said in that low, melodious tone.

He found her dulcet voice soothing, not the least shrill or grating.

"The sheriff has been away," she said, "so we could not ask him to put the word out on your behalf, either."

At her mention of the sheriff, a wave of icy dread sent a shiver rippling over him.

She glanced over her shoulder, and a shadow passed across her features.

"In truth, I was not certain you would survive. Neither was Charles—the physician who lives here and has a vested interest in the children's home. I am quite relieved that you have finally awoken."

"Thank..." He cleared his throat, the bile yet burning a scalding trail from his stomach. He managed a hoarse whisper. "Thank...you."

What else did one say when one could not remember how they had come to be unconscious in her meadow?

"Forgive me." She swept to the commode and poured a glass of water. Passing it to him, she said, "The cool water from our well should soothe your throat. Sip it slowly so you do not upset your stomach further."

He almost sighed aloud as the sweet water eased the acrid burning.

Sweeping his gaze over her face as he drank, he recognized the few small scars on her cheeks for what they were: pockmarks.

Not a lot and not severe, but noticeable regardless.

Pity filled him.

The world did not look kindly upon the flawed or imperfect in form, figure, or appearance.

He had firsthand experience in that regard.

How often had people gawked, or children shrank away in fear, at his eyepatch?

A rustling in the corridor alerted them to another's presence.

Before he finished drinking the blessedly cool water, a small, mouse-like elderly woman wearing spectacles and a gaudy knitted red shawl draped around her narrow shoulders over her nightdress, entered beside a tall, lanky young man who, from his disheveled appearance, had hastily donned his trousers and shirt.

Not only was his shirt inside out, but he held his trousers up with one bony hand.

"Ah, you are awake, at last. Excellent. I am Doctor Charles Montrose."

Surely not.

He squinted at the newcomer.

The fellow did not look old enough to have completed university, let alone medical studies.

Did he even boast whiskers yet?

The man peered harder.

Yes. There.

The merest shadow topped the doctor's upper lip, but those sparse hairs scarcely counted.

He had seen women with more impressive mustaches.

I have?

Not European women.

That must mean he had traveled somewhere exotic.

He tucked that tidbit into a corner to examine later.

Who knew what little detail might prove useful in jogging his memory?

The good doctor strode forward, seemingly not the least disturbed or concerned about his unkempt appearance. Or that his trousers were in danger of slipping off his skinny bum.

"You gave us quite a fright, I tell you." His free hand on

his hip, eyes narrowed, and mouth taut, the doctor gave a slow nod of approval. "I believe the worst is behind us, though you still have quite a recovery ahead of you. A less stalwart chap would not have survived, I dare say."

A smile teased the corners of his mouth when he took in the awful nightshirt.

Not his, then.

"I shall put the kettle on now. The children will be about soon enough, in any event." The elderly woman produced a cheerful smile, revealing several missing teeth. Her keen gaze bored into him. "A bit of gruel too, I should think. Nothing too robust though. Your stomach cannot handle solid food just yet."

The man cleared his throat.

"May I inquire who you are?" he asked, since no introduction seemed to be forthcoming, and he could not very well call her Tiny Mouse Woman.

Blue eyes twinkling, she grinned. "Maudie Bletchley, but everyone calls me Mrs. B."

With that surname, he could well understand why.

"Now we shall finally know who our patient is." She adjusted the godawful shawl—probably a castoff donated to the home. "We had no choice but to burn your clothing. However, even filthy and tattered, they conveyed quality and refinement, as does your speech."

"You rambled a great deal in your delirium," Miss Granger put in by way of an explanation. "Though, truth be told, much of what you said was not distinguishable, and what was, made no sense."

"Indeed. A great deal of blathering, shouting, and swearing." Without missing a beat, Mrs. B continued. "Your eyepatch suggests you are a military or seagoing lad."

Hardly a lad.

Perceptive deductions, but were they accurate?

"Your name, good sir?" The petite woman held no qualms about prying, it seemed.

Three pairs of eyes gazed at him kindly but expectantly.

"I am..." He racked his brain for a name. "That is, I am..."

Devil take it.

Who am I?

He opened his mouth again, then snapped his shut.

Well, this is beyond troublesome.

Forehead furrowed as he stared at the coverlet, he piled through the archives of his mind for any sign of who he was. Any vestige of a memory or recollection that might help him with his identity.

Not a single name or nuance came to mind.

Not even the merest wisp.

He had absolutely no clue what his name was.

Amnesia. Blast it all.

He had amnesia.

At last, he accepted the harsh truth, and shrugging, raised an apologetic gaze.

"Unfortunately, I cannot tell you who I am."

What a bloody, sodding inconvenience.

"O-oh?" Mrs. B drew the exclamation out into two syllables, her voice raising an octave on the last.

Miss Granger and Dr. Montrose regarded him with mild concern.

He produced a cynical smile. "I regret that at present, I possess no memory beyond the moments before I collapsed in the meadow."

THREE

Kelston Hall Children's Home's welcoming kitchen

Almost three in the afternoon that same day

Lilly placed the last bread dough rounds in the oven before brushing the flour from her starched white apron and rolling her sleeves down.

She gave an appreciative sniff.

Aromatic herbs, including lavender, basil, fennel, and oregano grown on the estate hung on hooks suspended from the ceiling to dry, adding to the already appealing aromas of fresh bread, stew, and apple pie.

She rarely lent a hand in the kitchen anymore, but two of the part-time scullery maids—sisters—had sent word they were abed with influenza. To avoid infecting the children, Lilly implemented a strict rule: sick employees were not welcome on the grounds.

Ailing teachers must remain confined to their bedchambers until they had recovered.

It was impossible for Mrs. B and Florence—the other part-time maid—to prepare three meals for five and forty mouths as well as do the baking, food preparation, wash dishes, attend the laundry, and the many other tasks required in the kitchen, and to maintain the rest of the house.

Even though the teachers kept their bedchamber and classroom clean, as well as pitched in wherever else the current situation required, there never seemed to be enough bodies to get everything completed.

So, Mrs. B had recruited Lilly to help with the baking this afternoon, or else they faced a week of breadless meals. Not an ideal situation when feeding so many.

Smiling, Lilly untied her apron.

Honestly, she did not mind baking. She found the task a pleasant reprieve from the never-ending paperwork sitting atop her desk. Besides, she had plenty of experience cooking and baking. As a child in this same orphanage, Lilly had been assigned kitchen duties by the former headmistress.

However, unlike most of her childhood, where chore after chore filled every moment not spent on lessons, the children at Kelston Hall Children's Home today enjoyed more free time after their studies. Lilly insisted upon it when she had become the director and the headmistress eight years ago.

Besides traditional education, every child also engaged in swimming, archery, dancing, art, music, decorum, and riding lessons. The girls also received cooking, sewing, and medicinal herbs instructions, while the boys learned basic animal husbandry, agriculture, and carpentry skills.

Thus, when the time came to leave Kelston Hall at eighteen, the orphans would be better prepared to enter the world and find employment.

While running an organization of this size certainly benefited from, and required, the children's help to operate efficiently, Lilly took care not to exploit the orphans. Not only were they allowed to have fun, but she also encouraged games and play within appropriate boundaries and with adequate supervision, of course.

Six and thirty children, ranging in age from five to sixteen, running amuck on the estate's fourteen acres, which included several gardens, a small pond, an orchard, as well as livestock, and poultry, would not make for happy neighbors.

She could not afford to offend the nobility flanking Kelston Hall on three sides.

This manor, too, had once been an aristocrat's country home.

Beaumont Davenport, Viscount of Merrivale, once owned Kelston Hall. When the viscountcy had fallen upon hard times a few decades ago, his lordship sold the unentailed manor house, gaining him respite from debtors' prison.

His spinster elder sister bought the grand home.

Perchance, Matilda Davenport had possessed fond childhood memories of the slightly run-down manor and grounds.

In any event, she had founded Kelston Hall Children's Home six and thirty years ago and had overseen the school's administration until her death. The children highly anticipated her annual visits and receiving the sweets, small gifts, and new clothing Miss Davenport always provided.

To this day, Lilly remained partial to licorice drops.

Even Mrs. Edna Reubins, the former director, and her second in command, Miss Jane Brewer, put on their polite public façade for Miss Davenport's annual appearances. Of course, the moment their benefactor left, Mrs. Reubins and Miss Brewer reverted to their true natures: punitive, lazy, miserly, and spiteful.

Miss Davenport had insisted Mrs. Reubins hire Lilly as a teacher at just sixteen—the age most children left Kelston Hall back then. Lilly would be forever grateful to the dame for her kindness and favor.

Unwilling to lose her position or Miss Davenport's funding, Mrs. Reubins grudgingly complied, but she made sure Lilly knew she resented the appointment.

Even eight years later, Lilly still could not quite believe Miss Davenport had bequeathed her and Charles Kelston Hall as well as the dear lady's remaining fortune. That was after paying for Charles to attend medical school.

Yes, Miss Davenport had been a gentle, generous soul.

So sad she had never married or had children.

One of Lilly's first tasks as director had been to send sour-faced Mrs. Reubins and her sycophant, Miss Brewer, packing. Lilly replaced the mean-spirited women with kinder but firm, intelligent instructors who made educating and loving the children their utmost priority.

With careful management, wise economizing, and by utilizing the estate grounds to diversify income, Kelston Hall Children's Home had become self-sufficient and financially independent.

Not that Lilly did not appreciate donations to the home, whether financial or of some other means. She was not one to look a gift horse in the mouth. Any extra funds or supplies made it possible to enhance the children's education.

"I have a meeting with the sheriff at three Mrs. B, and I would like to look in on our patient before then to check on his progress. Perhaps, he has remembered something of importance that I can relay to Sheriff Wrottesley."

There had been no point in contacting the sheriff before now; not only had he been out of town until three days ago, but Lilly had no information about their patient that could help identify him.

Truth be told, every time she had contemplated contacting the sheriff before, wariness and reluctance had made her stomach sink. However, once the mystery man had awakened, she could no longer delay the inevitable.

Perchance, Mr. Clement Wrottesley could uncover who the chap was.

Or at least, piece together enough information about the stranger to place announcements in Prudhoe and the neighboring communities. However, it was too soon to distribute notices with a sketch of the injured guest.

Though fading, colorful bruises, as well as numerous scabs, still covered his severely battered face. The swelling had not completely abated, either. Likely, he needed to heal another week or so before she could attempt to capture his likeness on paper.

"I trust you can watch the loaves of bread and remove them from the oven, Mrs. B?"

Lilly glanced out one of the arched kitchen windows just in time to see Joseph Boone, Miles White, and George Newcomb begin lobbing the potatoes they had dug up at one another.

"Of course, dearie."

Mrs. B stood on a stool before the new cast iron stove and stirred an enormous pot of beef stew. She stepped down and brushed the back of her hand across her damp forehead.

"Excuse me just a moment, Mrs. B."

Lilly rushed to the door and threw it open.

"Gent-le-men!" She enunciated each syllable.

At once, the three boys froze with the potatoes in their dirty hands, their mischievous grins fading into guilty I-have-been-caught-red-handed expressions.

"We eat those potatoes. They are our food throughout the winter." Lilly gave each lad a hard stare. "I know *I* do not like bruised potatoes. What's more, damaged potatoes rot. I also do not like going hungry because our potatoes have spoiled."

Not that the children would ever go hungry.

However, they could certainly eat bread and gruel for a few meals to learn their lesson about wastefulness.

"We are sorry, Miss Granger." The eldest, and no doubt the instigator, Miles, dropped a tuberous missile at his dust-covered feet. The vegetable bounced once, then rolled to a stop next to the potato plant mound from whence it had emerged minutes before.

He brushed his soiled palms on his thighs several times, and Lilly hid a wince as he left dirt streaks on his trousers.

Those marks would not come out easily.

The epitome of solemn chastisement, Joseph nodded.

"Yeth," he lisped, wiping his fingers beneath his freckled nose and leaving a trail resembling a dirt mustache. "It shall not happen again, Mith Gwanger. I pwomith."

His face set in determined lines, George silently set about gathering the miniature cannonballs and placing them in a neat pile.

"Very well." Lilly gave a firm nod. "I shall deem this matter settled. Please make better choices in the future, boys. Now go wash up and spend the next hour reading your chosen novels in the library. I shall be along shortly to ask you about your books."

"Yes, Miss Granger," the lads chorused in unison before tearing off, no doubt grateful for the reprieve.

Perhaps, they had *too* much free time.

By the by, where was Miss Sanders?

The boys were supposed to be under her supervision and, had they been, the potato battle would never have commenced.

Shaking her head and forehead puckered, Lilly shut the door.

"I thought Miss Sanders said she intended to take the younger students bird-watching this afternoon, Mrs. B."

Mrs. B made a disapproving sound in her throat before pinching her mouth tight as if she struggled to restrain herself before finally blurting, "I would wager my best bonnet she has sneaked off to flirt with the Mansfield's groom. *Again*. Likely, she pawned her charges off on Miss McKenzie. Miss McKenzie frets about the children too much to say no to the imposition."

Lilly puffed out a breath from between her lips.

If Mrs. B said Miss Sanders was hieing off for clandestine meetings, then that was that. Any gossip or tattle within five miles, and Mrs. B knew all the sordid details. Not that Lilly listened to tattle regularly, but the truth was, Mrs. B knew just about everything that went on.

Hence, Miss Ruby Sanders was not long for Kelston Hall.

Lilly must admit, hiring her had proved a mistake, despite her stellar references.

In the seven months the woman had been here, she had proven lackadaisical and inefficient. This was not her first inappropriate liaison either—which meant Lilly had no choice but to terminate her employment and post the position. It also meant rearranging the other staff's schedules and likely having to teach lessons herself in the interim.

Even if deserved, Lilly disliked giving anyone their congé.

However, the children's home had a reputation to uphold. Teachers who shirked their duties and failed to be good moral examples to the children could not remain.

Miss Sanders, too, should have made better choices.

Just one more unpleasant thing Lilly must deal with today.

Mrs. B gave her an encouraging smile.

"Thank you for the help, Lilly. Hopefully, Sheriff Wrottesley can shed a little light on who our mysterious guest is."

"I enjoyed making the bread." And Lilly had.

Should the good Lord have seen fit to allow her to marry and have children, Lilly quite thought she would have liked cooking and baking for her family.

Fully in command of her kitchen, Mrs. B waved her wooden spoon in the air, like a monarch wielding her scepter.

"Make sure to leave the office door open, and I shall have a lass bring you a cup of tea as an excuse to make sure the bounder does not dare cross the mark." She cackled, unashamed of her missing teeth. "Or I can come myself, rolling pin in hand to defend your honor."

Lilly grinned as she imagined that scene.

Mrs. B winked. "You could always wave your pistol in his arrogant face."

FOUR

Still in the fragrant kitchen

Lilly chuckled. "Let's hope that will not be necessary."

Mrs. B had been at Kelston Hall almost as long as Lilly had. What was more, she knew Wrottesley was a lecherous toad. No female under the age of eighty, save the most powerful and influential, were safe from the wretch's unwanted attentions.

Lilly kept a pistol and a blade in her desk drawer—just in case he overstepped.

Men like Wrottesley should never hold powerful positions.

The sheriff turned a blind eye to the nefarious actions his cronies committed while accepting bribes, practicing extortion, and acting a tyrant toward anyone who dared cross him. But as the local magistrate's brother-in-law, the likelihood of Sheriff Wrottesley getting his comeuppance was as probable as Lilly marrying nobility.

Marrying at all, for that matter.

It would not happen.

Poor, orphaned, with ugly scars upon her face, and long on the shelf, she had rarely entertained the notion of marriage anymore, which was another reason she had been so grateful to Miss Davenport for ensuring Lilly had a position at Kelston Hall Children's Home.

Each month, Lilly tucked away a percentage of her wages for her dotage, for she knew well that the day would come when she must step aside so a younger, more energetic woman could take her place.

Still, that time was decades away, and meanwhile, she had a school to run and a stranger to identify.

His family must be worried sick.

Sparing a couple of seconds before the corridor's simple convex mirror, she tucked a few stray hairs back into place, brushed a dab of flour from her chin, and pinched a bit of color into her cheeks.

As director of the school, she must always present herself as a professional.

Even to strangers suffering from amnesia.

As she climbed the stairs to the third floor, she considered the man.

As most of the children already slept two to a bed, and she could hardly shove Mrs. B from her narrow cot, Lilly, always pragmatic, had opted to sleep on the floor in her bedchamber with the door open.

Besides, someone needed to monitor the invalid. Particularly those first few days when it had been touch-and-go, and his life had hung in the balance.

Kind and generous as always, Dear Charles had offered Lilly his bedchamber. But often, calls kept him out all night, and he needed to sleep in his chamber when he returned. She had become quite proficient at dressing behind a screen in her office, but now that the stranger had awoken, she would need to find somewhere else to sleep.

The short, narrow settee in the office did not appeal.

Another sigh escaped her.

A makeshift bed on the office floor seemed her only option.

Giving a brief knock on the doorframe, she shoved the partially open door to her bedchamber wide and strode inside.

Hawkish eyebrows a stark contrast to his pallid face, her guest lay with his hands resting atop his belly, his eye closed. The black patch covering his other eye had known better days.

She had never seen that eye—because he had been unconscious when they hauled him into the house, and after washing his face and treating his wounds, she had replaced the eyepatch.

Somehow, she had sensed it would be important to him—to his dignity—to keep the damaged eye covered. Nevertheless, she could not quite subdue her curiosity about how he had come by the injury or what his eye looked like.

Even bruised and swollen, the contours of his rugged face fairly screamed refinement.

Who, precisely, was this mysterious man?

Surely, he was not a criminal or an escaped convict?

Was he?

Her stomach flopped over, and she pressed a hand to her tumultuous middle at the unwelcome thought.

Calm down, Lilibet Vivian Summer Granger, she ordered herself sternly. *This is not the time for histrionics.*

Why hadn't she considered those possibilities earlier?

Because—*you dolt*—she had always had a soft spot for the less fortunate. Still, she had a duty to protect the children and staff.

Insensate and on the brink of death, the stranger had not been in any condition to pose a threat.

But now?

She must discover his identity with all due haste because in another week—maybe less—he might well be strong enough to leave her bed. Surely Wrottesley would know any criminals the authorities sought in the area, although handing the stranger over to the likes of Sheriff Wrottesley went against everything in her.

Even if this man was a thief.

Or worse.

Distinctly more wary than she had been upon entering her room, Lilly eyed her uninvited guest.

How did one know if a person was a rotter?

A handsome man who many women considered quite dashing, the sheriff's outer appearance hid a vile soul and black character. So just because this man did not look evil, did not mean he was not.

She shifted her focus to his eyepatch.

Was that a clue?

Mayhap Mrs. B was wrong.

Perhaps, he had not been in the military or was not a man of the sea at all, but a highwayman or a footpad.

Lilly's heart skipped a beat, and her mouth went dry as sawdust.

She cast a swift glance at the stout paneled door.

Perhaps, she should start locking the chamber.

Just in case.

Yes. Yes, that was what she would do.

He could not escape out a window from the third-story bedchamber without breaking his neck. As she had already removed most of her clothing and was not sleeping in her chamber until he left, that seemed the most sensible solution.

Having come to that logical decision, Lilly felt much reassured, and she breathed out a silent sigh of relief, though a tiny stab of remorse pricked her at her inhospitable musings.

As he appeared fast asleep, her questions would have to wait, which meant further delay in discovering just who this man was. She collected the key from its cozy mooring inside the lock. The metal made a faint scraping noise, and she made a mental note to have all the keyholes in the house oiled since she could not recall when they had last been attended to.

"I am awake."

She almost yelped in surprise. Only years of having naughty children pull pranks on her kept her face serene and her composure sedate.

Lilly pivoted as he slowly opened his eye.

Unrelenting flinty gray bored into her before dropping to the skeleton key clutched between her thumb and forefinger. This was not a man one wanted as an enemy, and what she intended to do would make him hers.

A shiver scuttled across her shoulders.

"So, I am to be a prisoner now?"

FIVE

Still in Miss Granger's bedchamber

After the passage of several harrowing heartbeats

The flush sweeping up the slope of Miss Granger's gently rounded cheeks and her small tongue darting out to dampen the plump pillow of her lower lip confirmed her guilt.

Not that he blamed her.

If he did not know who the devil a person was, he would bloody well lock them inside a room too.

For all he knew, he might be a smuggler or a swindler.

Or worse.

The simple slate blue gown she wore did nothing to enhance her features, but neither did it detract from her natural attractiveness.

She possessed a refreshing, unpretentious allure.

Like a summer wildflower-filled meadow.

Yes, indeed. Miss Lilibet Granger resembled an overlooked wildflower.

A bluebell, or perhaps a campion, or a poppy.

Egads, man.

You are as frail as a flower petal yourself, and yet you are indulging in flights of fancy over a woman you have known mere hours?

He summoned what he hoped was a reassuring smile.

Or at least he tried to.

His still-healing, scabbed-over mouth did not permit a genuine smile, and he suspected he must rather resemble a gargoyle on Osterley Park House.

"You need not look so chagrined, Miss Granger."

With some effort, he levered himself into a sitting position. "Were I in your position, I would err on the side of caution too."

"I am sorry, but prudence must dictate." Giving a small nod, she ventured a few feet nearer the bed. "I know nothing about you, and until I do..." She lifted one shoulder. "Surely you understand."

Her gaze held compassion but also unwavering determination.

"I assure you, I am not offended because you have decided to lock the door." He grimaced as a rib protested his movements. "Though, I might go out of my mind with boredom."

"I can offer an extensive selection of books if you feel up to reading," she said. "I also subscribe to *The Times*, but delivery is delayed three days. We are always a tad behind on recent events and news."

That minor detail raised her another notch in his estimation. Most women had no interest in news sheets, preferring gossip rags such as *La Belle Assemblée, Le Beau Monde-Literary and Fashionable Magazine,* or *High Life in London.*

How the bloody hell do I know the names of women's periodicals?

"Although..." A frown creased Miss Granger's normally

smooth forehead. "You should take care to get sufficient rest so you do not prolong your recovery."

A polite way of saying, she did not want him convalescing at her children's home for months. And by God, he did not want to, either. He was every bit as eager as she to discover who he was and be on his way.

"Something to read would be appreciated." In truth, he was not positive he was up to the task just yet. Even this brief conversation had taken a toll and, exhaustion weighing his eyelids, he slumped into the pillows.

As she had done this morning, she rested her hand atop the footboard. A few ink stains marred her fingertips.

"Perhaps, I should get a pen and paper, so you can jot down any thoughts or memories that come to mind that may be useful." Hesitating, she ran her keen regard over him. "Or, I can do it if you are not feeling quite the thing, just yet."

Miss Granger had noticed his failing strength.

He gave a slow nod, careful not to jostle his head.

Thank God the pulsating agony of this morning had passed and now a dull throbbing ache encircled his skull.

"I have just recalled something about Osterley Park House." He stifled a yawn.

"*Hmm*, that might be rather useful." Attention focused on her hands, she scrunched her pert nose in concentration. "If I recall correctly, Osterley Park House is owned by the Earl of Jersey."

She raised her inquisitive gaze to meet his. "Yes?"

He could not prevent his eyebrows from shooting high on his forehead in surprise at her knowledge. "Yes, indeed."

"I am somewhat of an architectural buff." Miss Granger stared out the window, a hint of forlornness shadowing her features. "Had my circumstances been different, and had I been born a male, I should have liked to have pursued a career in architecture."

Unexpected empathy filled him.

She lifted a rounded shoulder again, a movement he was coming to recognize as her way of saying she did not care when she did.

"*C'est la vi.*" The merest trace of regret threaded her voice.

True, life did not always go as one wanted or thought it would.

For he had certainly never planned on being abducted, beaten to a pulp, suffering from amnesia, and being a burden to a children's school director.

Eyes narrowed in thought, Miss Granger put a finger to her chin. "The Countess of Jersey is an Almack peeress, is she not?"

"Is she?" How the blazes did he know? "However, I think I may have connections to the *haut ton* or know people who do."

"Excellent." Her smile might have been fashioned for a child who had, at last, mastered their multiplications.

"Let's write down everything that you can recall, shall we?" she said. "Mayhap a pattern will emerge."

She skirted the bed and then lifted the slanted cover to her secretary. After removing a sheet of foolscap, she opened her inkwell and dipped a pen into the ink.

A ray of sun filtering through the window cast her in a golden glow.

Why did she seem to grow prettier by the minute?

Even the few pockmarks on her cheeks appeared less noticeable. In truth, artfully applied cosmetics might conceal the shallow scars completely.

How do I know anything about cosmetics?

Do I have sisters?

Does my mother use paints?

Perhaps, I am acquainted with actresses.

And who did he know who wore lavender?

For that matter, how did he know about herbs' medicinal smells?

"It is a place to start, I suppose," he ventured, still uncertain anything he had recalled so far was of genuine worth in the quest to identify him.

"Well?" She arched an expectant eyebrow. "What have you remembered?"

He sighed. "We have already determined I know something of Osterley Park House."

"Yes, indeed." She scratched away on the foolscap, her lips pressed into a tight ribbon. "Very telling, I should think."

He wished he were as confident as she was.

It would help if he could speak with Doctor Montrose and ask him how long he could expect to wait to have his memory fully restored.

"What else?" she gently probed.

"I believe I was in the military—a soldier. Perhaps, an officer." He gestured toward his eyepatch. "I am not sure how I acquired this, however. I know I was beaten, but I do not know where or by whom."

"*Uh, hum.*" With her lower lip clamped between her teeth, she recorded the details.

He brushed his bandaged hand along his jaw, wincing as the rough bristles caught the cloth.

Lord, he needed a shave.

"I think..." Yes, he was almost certain. "I think I may have been abducted."

"*Pardon?*" she gasped, her flabbergasted gaze flying up to meet his. "You are certain?"

Was that genuine concern in her brown eyes, or did doubt linger in her irises?

He paused for a couple of heartbeats before giving a tentative nod. "Yes. Again, I do not know by whom or why."

"Well, that certainly puts things in a different perspective."

Miss Granger quickly recorded that tidbit before pausing and staring at the list. "Surely if you have been abducted, someone is looking for you. Unless..."

She raised an apologetic gaze to his. "Unless you do not have anyone."

"Honestly, I do not know."

Did he have anyone?

If so, why had no one found him in the fortnight he had been in residence at Kelston Hall Children's Home?

Almost immediately, she shook her head, dismissing the idea.

"No, that makes no sense. Abductions are usually committed to extort money." Lips pursed, she narrowed her eyes. "That leads me to venture you are related to someone who possesses wealth or position. Perhaps both."

"I sincerely do not know. However, I am familiar with the trappings and goings-on of the *haut ton*. I also have an unusual knowledge of women's cosmetics and periodicals. And the fragrance of lavender is very familiar to me, as are some herbs you have used to treat my injuries."

"*Cosmetics?*" Miss Granger could not hide her staggered expression. "That is certainly...uncommon."

She obviously understood that other than actresses, courtesans, and aristocrats—the latter, discreetly, of course—most women did not use beauty enhancements.

That meant he either had disreputable or prestigious female acquaintances.

The speculative look she slid him seemed to try to see inside his head to determine which was the case.

"I also have a vague recollection of a black-and-white-tiled marble foyer," he blurted to point her discomfiting, contemplative musings in another direction.

He sure as Hades was not mentioning that he believed he

normally slept naked. No need to share that shocking detail with the proper Miss Granger.

Except, damn him for a rogue, he rather thought he would enjoy seeing color flood her face.

After setting aside the pen, she held the list up. "I believe we have the beginnings of a picture here. Granted, it is not clear, by any means, but there are enough details that I think when I present them to Sheriff Wrottesley this afternoon, he might start to put the pieces together."

"Sheriff Wrottesley?" A stab of alarm speared him.

It made no earthly sense, but his intuition shrieked, "*Caution! Caution!*"

"Is he an honest fellow?" He pressed his lips tight for a heartbeat. "Someone you would trust?"

She grew pensive and averted her gaze as she waved the foolscap to dry the ink.

Finally, she shook her head. Not one lustrous, golden hair in her tightly coiled chignon quivered at the movement. "No, he is not what I consider an honorable man. Furthermore, I do not trust him in the least. I think..."

She inhaled a deep breath, and he truly tried to ignore the enticing rise of her well-endowed bosom.

"I think it would be wisest to not alert the sheriff to your presence just yet, though how I shall explain why I asked him to call this afternoon, is rather a pickle.

"What is more, the children, Charles, and the staff know you are here.

"It would not surprise me at all if Sheriff Wrottesley is not already aware you are here. In small communities, it is hard to keep secrets."

"Especially since you did not think you needed to." He gave a slow nod. "Perhaps, there is no need to tell him I have regained consciousness just yet."

She considered that for a moment.

"Perhaps, but I cannot make any promises. I shall not lie. However, I shall not offer him information either." She tilted her head. "It does make me wonder all the more whether you are a blackguard and are faking your memory loss."

He burst out laughing, immediately regretting it when his head nearly exploded. Cradling his throbbing skull between his hands, he gave her a cocky grin. "Are you always so suspicious, or do you simply have an over-active imagination?"

Crossing her arms, she speared him with a thunderous glare.

"Until I know what manner of man you are, I shall make no apologies for my qualms. And just because I am not handing you over to the sheriff today does not mean I shall not tomorrow. Understood?"

He felt rather like a chastened schoolboy. "Aye."

Beneath her calm exterior, Miss Lilibet Granger was a spitfire.

Very interesting.

And intriguing.

"Good." Stiff with disapproval and offense, she strode to the door. "I suggest you concentrate on regaining your memory and pray that you are not a miscreant. Know this: I shall do nothing to endanger the children or my staff.

"Nothing! If that means rendering you into the custody of the sheriff before you are fully recovered, I shall do so."

With that fierce declaration, she shut the door, and a second later, the key scratched in the lock.

He sank back into the pillows.

That had not gone brilliantly, and he had forgotten to ask for a different nightshirt.

Sighing in self-disgust, he closed his eyes.

Who the bloody hell am I?

SIX

Kelston Hall Children's Home
Lilly's office

Still the same day—quarter before four in the afternoon

Where is he?

For at least the fifth time in the past forty-five minutes, Lilly nudged aside the lace curtain with her bent forefinger and examined Kelston Hall's circular paved stone drive.

Sheriff Wrottesley had not come.

Neither had the inconsiderate lawman sent an excuse by messenger.

True, as the county's high sheriff, Wrottesley's duties took him to villages, towns, and hamlets all over Northumberland.

That is *when* he fulfilled his duties.

Most of the time, he simply did as he pleased, and none dared complain for fear of retribution. Only the good Lord knew where the cur was today or why he had not kept his appointment.

"Enough of this."

She let the age-yellowed panel slide back into place, where the lace swished against the decades-old, faded bronze damask draperies.

How Lilly despised the color and the musty old hangings.

Yet she could not justify splurging for new draperies, even of a less expensive fabric such as chintz or velvet, when these fusty old hangings sufficed.

On rare occasions when she permitted herself to daydream, she imagined glorious, colorful brocade draperies and furnishings.

Bold and daring.

Nothing drab or neutral.

Crimson red, royal blue, or emerald green.

In truth, she preferred brighter, lighter tones for her gowns as well, but headmistresses could hardly flit about the children's home wearing pinks, corals, or periwinkle, could they?

Who would take her seriously if she did not dress the part?

Lilly gave a firm shake of her head to dispel her fanciful musing.

She had tasks to see to.

Three mischievous little chaps awaited her to check their reading progress, and she must dismiss a neglectful teacher.

Never one to waste time, Lilly filled the last three-quarters of an hour by responding to correspondences and writing an advert for the soon-to-be-open teaching position.

Blast Miss Sanders for being lackadaisical and dishonest.

A blank piece of foolscap lay atop Lilly's desk.

She replaced it in the fifty-year-old black walnut pedestal desk's top drawer. Something had checked her impulse, other than a hesitancy to part with the coin, to also place notices in two or three papers about the stranger in her chamber.

It was not as if someone had misplaced a reticule or riding crop at a house party.

This was a badly beaten, and according to him, abducted man.

Mayhap nefarious forces were at work, and the last thing she needed was to lead them straight to the children's home.

Arms folded, she drummed her fingertips on her upper arms.

Did that mean the home and children were in more danger than she had previously conceived?

In that case, her reluctance to make his presence widely known made absolutely no sense.

Unless he was telling the truth.

How could she possibly know?

Cross about her double-mindedness, she pulled her mouth into a tight line.

In point of fact, Lilly was disgusted with herself for not having better screened the teaching applicants. Miss Sanders had provided glowing references, which Lilly had painstakingly verified.

But then again, how could one really know someone else?

What circumstances might make a person behave in a manner they never would have normally?

That train of thought brought her focus back to the visitor above.

Well, at least she had not been compelled to weave a believable tale for the sheriff to explain why she had summoned him here.

Oddly relieved that Wrottesley had stood her up, she rubbed her nape for a few moments.

The hard floor made an unaccommodating mattress, and she had battled aching muscles and stiffness these past two weeks, which only reminded her she was not as young as she once was.

After placing the small stack of letters on the corner, she tidied up her already neat desk and with a last glance at the dressing screen which concealed the nook that would become her make-shift sleeping chamber for the indeterminable future, she left her office.

Having decided to speak with Miss Sanders straightaway, she made for the woman's third-story chamber. She would start the search there and continue with the rest of the house and grounds.

Men's laughter carried to Lilly as she approached the landing, and brow furrowed, she picked up her pace.

Charles and his patient?

Alarm sluiced through her when she turned the corner and observed her bedchamber door standing open.

Drat and double drat.

There had been no opportunity to speak with Charles about confining their uninvited guest.

Stupid, stupid numpty for leaving the key in the keyhole.

With more trepidation than the situation warranted, Lilly approached her chamber just as another round of laughter burst forth.

"I am sincerely grateful. All that lace did rather emasculate me."

Lilly peeked around the doorjamb just in time to see the donated nightshirt get tugged over the mysterious stranger's dark head, exposing a nicely muscled chest covered with a tempting smattering of sable hair. The strips around his ribs stood out in stark contrast to his tanned skin, suggesting he had spent time shirtless in some place that boasted considerably more sun than the English countryside.

She should add that detail to her list of clues about him.

"*Ahem.*" She cleared her throat and continued into the room. "What, may I ask, is going on?"

SEVEN

Still in Lilly's bedchamber

Ten awkward heartbeats later

CHARLES HALF-TURNED, a green and gold striped nightshirt clutched in his hands. Clothing rumpled and hair unkempt as usual, he gave her a sideways smile. "Our guest was less than comfortable wearing a matron's cast-off nightgown. I rummaged through the recent donations and found this."

He held the faded garment up.

It appeared too small, hence why she had selected the lacy nightgown. The previous owner must have been quite large. Finding a nightshirt that would accommodate his broad shoulders had been somewhat of a challenge, as had maneuvering the insensate man into the garment. As he had been unaware of his attire, Lilly had opted for pragmatism rather than fashion.

Lilly almost blurted, *Beggars cannot be choosers*, but held her tongue.

She conceded such a rugged man had looked rather silly with ruffled lace at his neck, wrists, and several rows across his chest. At least she had removed the slew of pink ribbons previously adorning the garment.

With a devilish twinkle in his eye, their guest looked over Charles's shoulder.

"I usually sleep nude, but in consideration of your tender sensibilities..." He trailed off, but a distinctly wicked gleam shone in his gray eye.

Of all the things to remember.

Flames licked her cheeks, but Lilly held his mocking stare.

Their invalid must be feeling better, the rogue.

Charles choked on a cough.

Or was it a chuckle?

In truth, Lilly was not sure which.

She leveled him a contemplative glance.

Surrounded as he was by women, from servants to teachers, Dear Charles likely relished a jot of masculine company.

"I assume we can chalk that tidbit up to another recalled memory?" Heat still scorched her cheeks, but Lilly refused to give their patient the satisfaction of averting her gaze.

She advanced farther into the room.

By Jove, he would not intimidate her or ruffle her composure.

She wore her poised comportment like a second skin—a requirement when dealing with children and difficult adults as well.

He chuckled, a pleasant rumbling deep in his chest, then grimaced as Charles swiftly slid the nightshirt over his head. It took several tries and as many minutes, accompanied by a series of grunts and low curses, to maneuver the patient's arms into the sleeping attire.

As she suspected, the fit was too tight.

To his credit, he did not complain but merely reclined against the pillows, the fabric straining over the muscles of his broad chest and broader shoulders. And revealing a shocking expanse of masculine chest at the vee created by the too-tight fit.

Even Lilly had to admit the nightshirt was a vast improvement over the frilly lady's nightgown.

Still, what did he think?

They had a variety of sleeping attire stored away for every scenario?

This was a children's home.

Nothing went to waste here.

The discarded nightdress would have been made into two or three nightgowns for little girls.

"Charles, may I have a word with you please?" she asked, careful to keep her tone professional and benign.

Pulling his eyebrows together into a puzzled vee, Charles nodded as he faced their *guest*.

"Please excuse me. I shall remove the bandages on your hands and head when I return." He grinned.

Yes, Charles was relishing the male company.

"Then we shall have that game of cards. Provided I do not get called out to see a patient," he said. "Your ribs will need to stay wrapped for at least another week."

"Thank you." Their patient responded to Charles, but his keen, steely gaze never left Lilly. "How did your meeting with the sheriff go, Miss Granger?"

Ah, he fretted she had revealed his presence.

Because he genuinely did not trust a man he had never met, or at least did not recall knowing, or because this whole amnesia business was a well-thought-out ruse?

Picking the castoff nightgown off the floor, Lilly straightened with it dangling from her fingertips. "It did not. He never arrived."

"Oh, bother." Slapping his forehead, Charles offered a sheepish smile.

"I completely forgot, Lil. Forgive me. This morning, I bumped into Wrottesley in Prudhoe.

"He said he had been called away on official business to Berwick-upon-Tweed this afternoon. Something to do with smugglers. He said he would be in touch when he returns."

Knowing the sheriff's propensity for corruption, Lilly bet Wrottesley wanted to ensure he received his cut of the booty.

Everyone knew of the smuggling that occurred along the North Sea coast.

With the many hidden coves and inlets, the geography was perfect for running illegal goods and avoiding customs fees and taxes. Plus, Berwick-upon-Tweed's proximity to the English-Scottish border provided an even more lucrative way to distribute the contraband.

She eyed the man lying in her bed.

Hmm, might *he* be a contrabandist?

With that eyepatch, he resembled a pirate.

And undisguised relief softened the hard contours of their patient's features.

"I suppose it is just as well for now." She tore her attention from the mystery man and seized Charles's arm, practically dragging him from the chamber.

Wearing a befuddled expression, Charles permitted her to tow him along.

After pulling the door closed behind them, she continued several feet down the corridor until she was certain the *prisoner* could not overhear them.

"Whatever has taken hold of you, Lil?" he asked, using his nickname for her since they had been children.

Despite not being related by blood, Charles was her

brother, and she was his sister, in every other way. Both had arrived at Kelston Hall as toddlers and, for whatever reason, Miss Davenport had taken a personal interest in them.

"*Shh*, Charles."

"Why was your chamber locked from the outside?" Charles scraped a hand through his already tousled locks. "And why is it just as well the sheriff did not pay a call today?"

"Please lower your voice, Charles." After assuring no children or staff lurked nearby, Lilly dropped her voice to a whisper. "It occurred to me today, that we literally know nothing about him."

She gave a pointed look at the closed door.

"For all we know, he might be a criminal." She drew herself up to her full height, all five feet seven inches. "So, I decided until we know exactly who our uninvited guest is, to protect everyone, my chamber shall remain locked. I explained my reasons to him earlier, and he was surprisingly amenable."

Cupping his nape, Charles scraped the toe of his shoe along the floorboard. "I s'pose you are right. He just does not strike me as the unsavory type, though."

"I understand, Charles." She peeked around again to ensure their privacy—a rare commodity with this many people under one roof. "However, appearances can be deceiving. What is more, he is extremely worried that I shall notify the sheriff that he is here, and he told me earlier that he believes he was abducted."

That jerked Charles's attention from the scuffed floor to Lilly's face. "Abducted?"

Nodding, she withdrew the paper where she had jotted the notes down about him earlier in the day, sans the additional detail: he slept nude. "Here is a list of things he can remember. It is not much, but there are some interesting details that might be useful to help identify him."

She passed the creased foolscap to Charles, who swiftly perused the short list.

A thoughtful expression crossed his face, and he wiggled the sheet in the air, causing it to rustle with the motion.

"May I have this? I believe I heard something several days ago in..." He frowned, in concentration, his eyes distant behind his spectacle lenses. "Devil take it, I cannot remember if it was in Hexham, Alnwick, or Morpeth. The tidbit did not register as important, but now..."

"Yes, you may have it. I can make another copy from memory." She glanced out the window and skimmed the land-scape—a habit from years of overseeing children.

Miss Sanders crept from the tree line, then dashed behind the henhouse.

From the corner of her eye, Lilly watched the teacher's stealthy progress until she disappeared around the back of the house. She was probably using the servants' entrance to sneak upstairs.

Well, Lilly would be waiting for her.

"I would wait to inform Wrottesley." Charles rubbed his chin. "We know he is an untrustworthy sot and that he takes bribes. If our friend," this time it was his turn to focus on the closed bedchamber door, "was indeed abducted, then Wrottesley may well know who was behind it, and in truth might be in cahoots with the blokes."

That thought had crossed Lilly's mind as well.

Arms folded, she tapped the toes of one foot. "And in the meanwhile, we do not know whether we can trust our *'guest'* in the least."

"He is still in no condition to be much of a threat," Charles assured her with a kind smile. "I promised him a game of cards this evening."

"Gads, I forgot." Chagrin stabbed Lilly. "I promised to

bring him a book or two and a few news sheets. I shall fetch them after I speak with Miss Sanders."

"Letting her go, are you?" Compassion darkened Charles's brown eyes.

Lilly cast him a surprised glance. "Yes, but how did you...?"

"She has been sneaking about for months, Lill." His gaze held sympathy. "You have just been too busy and too trusting to notice. I did not feel it was my place to inform you as long as the children were not neglected, that is."

"They have been neglected. Today, I caught three unsupervised boys having a potato war. Which makes me derelict in my duties as the home's headmistress and director." She stiffened her spine and jabbed her finger toward her chamber door. "Trust me when I say, I shall not make the same mistake with him. He will stay confined in my chamber until I am certain he is not a threat."

EIGHT

Lily's bedchamber at Kelston Hall

Half of nine that evening

A sharp rap upon the bedchamber door drew the man's attention from the dated news sheet just as the key ground in the lock. Grateful to have the use of his hands, sans their bandages, he had wasted no time in scouring several dated editions of *The Times* that Miss Granger had sent up with his dinner.

In truth, he had anticipated reading a snippet of something that would trigger his memory.

However, reports on the continued political pressure over Catholic emancipation as well as economic growth and industrial advancements did not spark so much as a tiny flame of recollection. Neither did the death of prominent figures or the fanfare about the upper ten thousands' social rounds.

The day had passed into evening with no additional insight into who he was, and it frustrated the devil out of him.

Was he a miscreant?

A bounder and a scoundrel?

He did not feel like a cad, but did crooks have consciences?

Did they know they were corrupt to their black souls?

Miss Granger toed the door open, then shoved it wide with her shoulder as she carried a lap tray into the bedchamber.

At once, his pulse quickened, and just as quickly, he subdued his carnal interest.

He was infirm—*had practically died, in truth*—and she was a prim and proper school director, for God's sake.

"Good evening."

She offered a half-smile, as if she was uncertain of her welcome.

Raising a mocking eyebrow in greeting, and with a slight rustle, he folded the papers before placing them on the night table.

"To what do I owe this unexpected pleasure?"

It startled him to realize it *was*, indeed, a pleasure to see her.

But then again, confined to a bed in a locked chamber, he was eager to see anyone. At least, he no longer wore the ridiculous ruffled nightgown.

"I have brought you a few things to help you sleep." She set the tray on the commode. "Warm milk, chamomile tea, and slices of buttered bread topped with strawberry jam."

He detested chamomile tea.

I do?

Probably not worth mentioning, so she could add it to her sleuthing list about him.

He would far prefer a dram or two of whisky or cognac. That would send him into the arms of Morpheus quite nicely, thank you. However, he rather doubted there was a drop of liquor in the entire house unless it was a bottle of cooking sherry.

Regardless, during his convalescence, he had lost a good deal of weight. Earlier, during their Piquet game, Charles recommended he eat several small meals until his stomach could handle larger quantities of food.

"I would drink the milk before it cools too much," Miss Granger advised. "The tea is quite hot still. I took the liberty of adding honey."

A smile tilted her mouth upward.

She was quite becoming when she smiled.

"Charles vows honey's medicinal qualities can cure almost anything."

She placed the tray on his lap, and once again, he caught a whiff of her unique scent. Not the cloying, heavy fragrances so many *ton* ladies preferred, but a refreshing and natural aroma, and perhaps, bearing the merest hint of yeast.

"Did you make the bread?" The words tumbled from his mouth before he registered them in his mind.

She was so close he could see the gold flecks in her doe-like eyes.

Her mouth parted in surprise, drawing his attention to her soft, full lips and breath smelling of tea and lemon.

Had she ever been kissed?

Egads, man. Control yourself.

Straightening, she nodded. "Actually, I did. I do not normally, but we were short two maids today."

"And the butter and jam?"

Why the bloody hell was he asking these inane questions?

Had he developed brain fever?

Had boredom muddled his mind?

No, it was the knock to his head. It had addled him.

There was no other explanation for his peculiar inquires.

Miss Granger's musical tinkle filled the chamber as she strode to her wardrobe and tossed the doors open. "Yes, I helped with the jam too, but not the butter. Although the cream came from Buttercup. The milk is from Clover."

"Ah, the brave lady bovines who rescued me, if I recall." He could not prevent his grin.

"Indeed." A smile twitched the corners of her mouth and sparkled in her eyes. "They are Jersey cows. Though at nine and eleven, respectively, their milk production is slowing a trifle."

Did her dulcet tone contain the merest hint of concern?

Less milk meant she might have to consider sending the old gals to the butcher and replacing them with younger cows. Somehow, he did not think Miss Granger was as pragmatic about her livestock as she was running her children's home.

Ducking her head inside the wardrobe, she rummaged around.

Outside, an owl hooted, the sound haunting and familiar.

Dutifully, he drank the milk, then gulped down the tea, wincing as the hot, sweet liquid burned his throat.

Godawful stuff.

He shuddered.

One might as well chew grass or nibble hay.

Cows and other herbivores were welcome to the stuff.

Standing back and staring at the wardrobe, Miss Granger planted her hands on her nicely rounded hips, a frown turning her mouth downward. "Where did I put the dashed thing?"

Taking a bite of the thickly sliced bread, slathered with creamy butter and delicious jam, he cocked his head. The muted light gave her an ethereal air, and he realized with a start, she was quite pretty.

Once he had swallowed, he said, "I take it you have misplaced something?"

"My valise." She sighed, even as she roved the chamber with her astute gaze. "I wanted to move more of my clothes and other possessions to the office, but I do not recall where I stored it. I rarely need luggage."

"I am sorry to be an inconvenience." A colossal pain in the arse, in truth.

A pang of guilt speared him.

His presence had caused her displacement. Charles mentioned she would sleep in the study now.

Still gazing about the chamber, Miss Granger flicked a hand in his direction. "It is hardly your fault, and I would do the same for anyone who needed help."

Yes, he rather believed she would.

A flash lit her eyes. "Aha! I remember now."

If only his memory would return as readily.

"I put it in the chest." She swiftly crossed to the end of the bed and dropped to her knees.

Chest?

What chest?

With a slice of scrumptious bread in one hand, he levered himself upward onto an elbow.

Indeed, a small wooden chest stood at the foot of the bed. He had not noticed it earlier because the footboard obstructed it from view and because it was not very tall.

She lifted the lid and, after pulling out several items, she released a satisfied, "Yes."

She proudly held up a dated, battered and, he would wager his tasty snack, what was a moth-eaten carpetbag.

Observing her as she gathered the items she wished to take below, he leaned back and finished his bread. She moved with an innate grace and lack of artifice.

When Miss Granger had finished, she set the stuffed-to-overflowing bag outside the open door, then returned to his bedside.

"You finished it all. Excellent." She collected the tray. "Charles and Mrs. B will be well-pleased."

And her?

"It was delicious. I did not realize how hungry I was." He wiped his mouth, then handed her the serviette. "Miss Granger?"

"Yes?" She gazed at him, her expression open and expectant.

Was she even capable of subterfuge?

He thought not.

"I think we need to give me a name for the time being." He lifted a shoulder. "It feels rather odd not to ever be addressed by a name."

"I imagine it is. Do you have a preference?" She wrinkled her nose. "Please do not say, 'John Doe.'"

A chuckle escaped him, for he was going to suggest John. "How about Zander? Is that unique enough for you?"

Where he came up with that name, he could not say.

"It is." She crossed to the door.

"Might I make one more request?" If he did not have a bath and a shave, he would go stark, raving mad. "I do not wish to be any more of an inconvenience than I already am, but is it possible for me to shave and bathe tomorrow?"

She angled her head. "I shall see what I can arrange. Tooth powder and a comb as well, I should think."

He liked that about her.

No immediate promises, vows, or claims.

Pragmatic and logical was Miss Lilibet Granger.

"Pleasant dreams...Zander."

The door closed with a soft snick and a second later, the key clunked the lock tight.

Laying back, Zander stared at the ceiling.

"If I dream of you, Lilly, they are sure to be sweet," he whispered to the still night.

NINE

Kelston Hall's drawing room

Nine days later—early afternoon

After another fruitless perusal that failed to jog a single memory, Zander uncrossed his knees and, sighing, snapped the news sheet closed. He tossed the well-read paper on the muted red and beige striped chintz settee beside him before bending forward and resting his elbows on his tweed covered knees, chin cradled on his fisted hands.

Staring into the unlit hearth, he tapped his toes, needing to expel the energy his healing body accumulated almost hourly. He might not remember his previous life, but he had not been a man of leisure, nor did he enjoy being idle or seden-tary now.

Three days ago, Lilly had lifted the order that he must remain locked in her chamber.

She did not give a reason, but Charles said she detested animals being confined in cages, much less humans, and he presumed Lilly had concluded after nearly another week that Zander did not pose a threat.

Giving the news sheet an undeserved, side-eyed glower, Zander plowed a hand through his hair.

One would think if someone went missing for weeks, a caring family would post adverts describing the missing person, where they were last known to have been, and perhaps even offer a reward, if financially feasible.

The papers remained conspicuously absent of any such notices, which led him to believe no one cared about his absence. Or, if he had any living family, they were too poor to place a notice in *The Times*.

Even as his physical body healed, his frustration grew.

It seemed he would need something substantially more powerful than outdated papers to regain his memory.

Who the blazes am I?

Over a week had passed, and he was no closer to discovering who he was than he had been when he had awoken.

Actually...that was not entirely true.

Over the past few days, hazy bits and bobs had filtered into his consciousness.

A petite, gaudily attired, bespeckled woman dripping with jewels and feathers.

A small, rundown cabin in the woods.

A snowball fight with grown men—and an auburn-haired a woman too.

Staring out the window, Zander blew out a long breath.

What did any of it mean?

What was more, he was bored out of his bloody mind.

This forced slothfulness grated more and more with each passing day. Thank God Lilly permitted him to wander the private part of the house as long as he avoided the children. She was adamant about that stricture.

Charles had approved Zander rising from his convalescence bed, but only if he continued to recuperate at a sedate pace.

No long treks outdoors.

Certainly no rigorous hikes, and heaven forbid that he go for a horseback ride or a swim.

How was he to discover who he was, confined to a few rooms in the house?

He may as well take up knitting, tatting, or embroidery.

Still, prowling about the local hamlets and villages probably was not the most prudent action. Not only might he encounter the sheriff—something he was not prepared to do just yet—it stood to reason, his abductors may well still lurk in the area.

Not that he would recognize them should he stumble upon the blighters.

All the more reason to stay put, as Lilly had calmly extolled two mornings ago when he had nearly begged like a two-year-old for an outing.

Fiend seize it.

Childish as it was, he could not hide a scowl and a pang of envy yesterday when four older children rode past the drawing room on their return to the stables.

What kind of orphanage provided riding lessons, among other unusual, but useful, training to the students?

A remarkable one.

Run by the extraordinary, forward-thinking Miss Lilibet Granger.

"I assure you, Miss Granger," a man intoned in a maddening, reedy voice that could have peeled paint from the ceiling, "I am most capable of instructing the children in geography, mathematics, and natural philosophy, and I am positive you will agree, my references are impeccable."

"So you have mentioned," Miss Granger replied. "I look forward to reading them."

Zander detected the merest hint of sarcasm in her dry response.

Another interviewee for the position recently vacated by the remiss Miss Sanders, according to Mrs. B. The cook had no qualms about tickling Zander's ears with the latest household and village gossip. And curse him for a twaddling fool. He looked forward to her chin-wagging sessions.

The old dear had imparted many interesting morsels.

Without a jot of compunction, he wandered to the doorway to earwig on the conversation between the potential teacher and Lilly. Peeking around the corner, Zander spied a long-faced chap with an impressive pair of sideburns the size of baby quokkas, but not nearly as adorable.

How the devil do I know what quokka is?

The fellow carried a well-oiled leather portfolio under one arm.

The sot looked and sounded like a humorless prig.

Precisely the sort of instructor children abhorred.

That made five—*no, six*—this week, but this chap was only the second male to apply for the position. Probably because most men did not like being accountable to a woman, and although Charles was part-owner of Kelston Hall Children's Home, he did not partake in the day-to-day operation of the orphanage and school.

Zander scratched his nose.

In truth, Charles and Miss Granger inheriting the place, was quite odd. Zander could not think if a single other instance where a peer simply deeded a manor to two orphans, but then again, his ability to recall anything relevant prior to his awakening, proved an irritating obstruction.

Mr. I-am-full-of-my-own-self-importance spoke again, and Zander winced.

God, that voice.

The children would hie for the hills with bits of rag stuffed in their ears just to escape his orations.

"As I mentioned in the interview, Miss Granger, my no-nonsense and stern approach to instruction and an occasional ruler across the knuckles for the worst-behaved students have served me well in my previous positions," the prig said.

Badly done, you boastful bully.

"I rarely have had to resort to the rod to enforce acceptable conduct. I believe in the biblical principle of spare the rod and spoil the child," He intoned with false piety.

The corners of Lilly's eyes flexed, and if the idiot had not been tooting his own horn, he would have noticed her displeasure. "Actually, that phrase is from *Hudibras*, a 17th century poem by Samuel Butler. The biblical verse you have mistaken it for emphasizes the importance of loving parents disciplining their children, and the rod is symbolic of guidance or correction, rather than literal, corporal punishment."

"Regretfully, you are mistaken, Miss Granger. For I also studied theology at university," argued the dimwitted candidate. "As I am certain you are aware, such subjects are reserved for *men's* superior intellect. It is understandable how *you* could have made such a mistake."

Zander's blood boiled at the thinly veiled insult.

The bloody, condescending, insolent jackanape.

Zander fisted his hands against the urge to rap his knuckles across the numbskull's weak jaw.

Miss Granger merely raised an eyebrow.

She is too smart to argue with a feckless fool.

The chap thrust out his unimpressive chest and jutted his almost absent chin atop his extraordinarily long neck, skyward.

The effect triggered another memory.

A long-necked turtle.

Where in the blazes had Zander seen such a thing?

The same place he had seen a quokka?

He should share these recent recollections with Lilly, but as they only created more questions, rather than the answers they both wanted, Zander would wait.

"I assure you. No one has ever said that Balthazar Drumblewick does not enforce discipline, both inside and outside the classroom," the boor bragged.

Zander stifled a snort.

Miss Granger fashioned what he recognized as her polite smile.

"Thank you, for coming, Mr. Drumblewick. I shall inform you once a decision has been made."

"*Erm*. Yes, of course." Drumblewick could not quite prevent his eyebrows from lashing together in disappointment.

Or...was that quickly masked look censure?

Zander narrowed his eyes.

Lilly's slightly elevated eyebrows revealed she had seen through the pompous windbag.

"I shall look forward to hearing from you. I can start as early as next week." Drumblewick bowed, and the shock of hair he had combed across his bald pate sprang loose from his pomade plastered head.

When he rose, the oily-waxy strand dangled near his ear like a hatchling snake.

To Miss Granger's credit, she did not so much as blink in surprise. Instead, she opened the door and held it for the disgruntled man.

Plastering the offensive, greasy strand across his head again, he gave a curt nod and then took his leave.

After closing the door, Lilly leaned against the stout panel. Lifting her face, she closed her eyes, appearing almost fragile in the filtered light.

"God give me strength. Isn't there a single qualified candidate who is not crack-brained?"

Zander could not contain his chuckle.

At once, she righted herself and glanced around suspiciously.

"Zander? Is that you?"

TEN

Kelston Hall's main corridor

After a handful of embarrassing heartbeats

Caught like a naughty lad in short pants.

Zander popped his head around the doorframe and offered an apologetic grin. "Guilty."

Wearing an odd assortment of borrowed clothing as well as donated cast-offs, he ambled forward.

"Explain yourself, please." The twinkle in Lilly's eyes belied her severe expression.

However, the stark, drab green gown she wore did nothing for her coloring. She should wear bottle or emerald green. Crimson and purple.

Even white would be more becoming.

He would wager as frugal as she was, she had bought the awful fabric at a discount.

And it was no wonder.

What woman chooses to wear pond-scum green?

"I shall not claim I did not mean to eavesdrop, Lilly

because once the twit opened his mouth, I fought the urge to hurry his exit from the house. What a condescending piece of sh—" Zander barely stifled the expletive. "Ah...cow excrement."

He really should not speak like that in a lady's presence, but with Lilly, Zander never had to pretend decorum he did not feel.

Lilly laughed, an unfettered ripple of pure joy, and he grinned in return.

"I said to myself that I would serve steaming cow patties at tea before hiring that...that..." she waved her hand toward the door.

"Turd?" Zander offered helpfully.

Eyes still sparkling with mirth, she nodded. "Indeed, although I would have called him a tosspot or snollygoster."

"How many interviews is that now, if you do not mind me asking?" Zander fell into step beside her.

Her shoulders slumped the merest bit before she squared them and lifted that pert chin.

Zander admired that about her.

Her gumption and intrepidness.

Lilly did not wallow in self-pity.

No, she was a problem-solver.

"All told, eleven. I am determined to not settle or rush into a decision and make another mistake like Miss Sanders again.

"I must find someone who is qualified, ethical, kind, but most of all, who loves children and understands them."

She pursed her lips.

"That blighter admitting he raps his students' knuckles or takes a rod to them, is, I assure you, *not* a good fit."

"I could do it." The words tumbled from Zanders' mouth, and while he had not planned on offering to instruct the students, he did not regret it either.

Have you lost your bloody, sodding mind?

"*You?*" Jaw slack, Lilly stopped short, gaping at him as if he had sprouted horns upon his head or grown another pair of eyes...This set, googly and bright purple.

Her total disbelief should not have stung as much as it did, but Zander did not examine why her incredulity chafed.

Holding his chin between his thumb and forefinger, he gave a thoughtful nod. "Yes. Me."

"You are teasing me." Shaking an ink-stained finger at him, she laughed again before continuing toward the corridor. "Very convincing, I must say. For a heartbeat, I almost believed you."

"I *could* do it," Zander persisted.

What was more, he wanted to. Not only would teaching provide him with something to do, but it would also give him a purpose.

Especially if he never regained his memory.

His mind shied away from that abhorrent thought.

He was not prepared to face that reality, just yet.

Unmasked skepticism radiated off her.

Well, then, reassure her, he would.

"I have always been fond of children..."

I have?

"I can teach all those subjects. I attended the University of Cambridge and graduated with First Class Honors and as a Second Wrangler."

That unexpected memory brought with it a rather smug sense of satisfaction.

Bully for me.

She swung her flaxen head toward him, eyes wide and mouth slack again. "Precisely when did you remember *that*, may I ask?"

"Just now, as we were speaking." He plowed a hand through his hair, then grinned. "Impressive, *eh?*"

"*Hmm*. Surely, there is a record of those accomplishments. I must write The University of Cambridge's registrar." Excitement and hope tempered with hesitation filled her gaze.

Which would win the internal battle?

And what if Lilly's inquiry proved successful, and she identified him?

What then?

Zander would finally know who he was.

But that could take weeks...months even.

Indeed, it could, and he would cross that bridge if, and when, the time came.

Eyes narrowed to slits so that only her irises showed, and her head canted sideways, Lilly clasped her hands together.

"I cannot believe I am even considering this for a second. Regardless, a male instructor would be ever so beneficial for the lads. Particularly a man who has experienced more in life than academics for the less scholarly-oriented boys." She tapped her chin with her forefinger, peering at him with such a penetrating stare, he felt she saw into his soul. "You would need a surname, of course."

Was she speaking to him or herself?

"I cannot allow the children to address you by a given name," she murmured.

Even if it is fake?

"Perhaps, Field since that is where we found you."

I think I would prefer Mr. Meadow.

It has a nice alliteration ring to it.

Wisdom cautioned Zander to keep silent and let her work through this her way, which appeared to be thinking aloud.

"You would have to take a timed examination first, Zander."

Lilly eyed him up and down, as if seeing him for the first time. "You must score in the ninetieth percentile or above in all three academic areas to qualify. It is a stringent requirement for employment, and I cannot make an exception for anyone."

"Fine." Summoning what he hoped was a charming smile, Zander crossed his arm over his chest in false gallantry. "I am at your disposal. Name the time and place."

How could he be so confident about this? He did not harbor a single doubt that he would perform well.

"Now." A challenging glint entered Lilly's brown eyes. "No time like the present. The last applicant canceled his interview. He has accepted a position elsewhere, so I have two free hours to oversee your examination."

Did she think Zander was not up to the task?

That he had boasted?

Had he?

Or that he needed time to study and refresh his knowledge?

Did he?

They would soon see.

"Very well." He lifted a shoulder, then extended his arm toward her study. "After you."

She marched ahead of him, spine ramrod straight, shoulders squared, and chin slightly elevated. But her rounded hips swayed nicely—*enticingly*—beneath the godawful fabric with each measured step.

Again, Zander's conscience railed him.

Have you lost what is left of your mind?

No.

Somehow, though it made no bloody sense, this felt right.

Almost... Almost as if destiny had placed him here at this exact time.

Except, he did not believe in fate or destiny or providence or any of that fanciful claptrap.

They reached her office, and once inside, Lilly closed the door. She faced him with the directness he appreciated.

"I have doubts as to the wisdom of this, Zander, and I usually listen to my intuition."

So did he, truth to tell.

"Let me complete the examination first, Lilly, and then we can discuss your concerns." He lifted a shoulder. "If I do not pass, they are moot anyway."

He scanned the orderly office.

A screen in the far corner partially hid her bedding, folded neatly on the floor.

A mule kick to his gut would have hurt less.

She slept there because of him.

It was past time he let her return to her bed.

"Have a seat there, please." She indicated a Pembroke table with one leaf lowered near a tall window. Indecision played across her features. "The children need stability. Once you remember who you are, Zander, you shall leave."

Perhaps.

Perhaps not.

Perchance, this is what he was meant to do.

Again, the nagging sensation that fate or providence was in play teased him.

Without a jot of regret or remorse, he dismissed the notion as drivel.

He took a seat at the table and asked the question plaguing him since awakening without his memory.

"What if I never remember, Lilly?"

ELEVEN

Four grueling hours later—late afternoon

One hand pressed to her forehead and an elbow resting on the desk, Lilly scored the examination for the third time.

She had not made a mistake.

Zander had passed.

Not only had he passed, he had excelled in every subject.

Only an imbecile would reject a candidate as academically qualified as he was.

How could a man not remember his name but could remember polynomial equations and caloric theory?

Fingertips pressed to her lips, Lilly relaxed against the chair back, her attention still focused on the examination papers.

Every instinct she possessed as a headmistress fairly screamed, "Retain him now!"

Zander would be an excellent asset to the children's home —at least academically.

Nevertheless, she could not shake the uneasiness that his leaving—and he would leave, of that she had no doubt— would cause gross disruption to the school, the students, the staff, and yes, if she were perfectly honest...to her life.

He was that kind of man.

One who made an extreme impression on everyone he met.

Charles could not stop raving about Zander's intellect, humor, and military knowledge.

Mrs. B was half in love with Zander and had taken to baking extravagant delicacies for him besides finding numerous excuses to chat with him throughout the day.

Even the part-time maids whispered behind their hands about the *tall, rugged stranger with the arresting gray eye,* and they, too, had feigned reasons to visit his chamber when he was still confined.

Now that he was not, the minxes arranged to *accidentally* run into him at every turn.

The shameless wantons.

If Lilly had an iota of common sense, she would send him packing.

Today.

But it seemed her levelheadedness had hied off to parts unknown and was not to be found.

Hadn't she let him out of her chamber when she had vowed she would not?

What was more, she permitted him the use of several rooms in the house.

Pure idiocy.

Not so foolish that she had allowed him to interact with the children or teachers, however.

The staff believed Charles nursed an injured traveler.

That was all.

The truth of it was, Lilly enjoyed Zander's company far more than she ought.

But if she hired him, how would she explain her decision to her fellow instructors?

Glancing at the exams one more time, she rose, then gathered the papers and slid them into a desk drawer.

Honestly, she had not considered he would pass the exams, let alone excel at them.

She had merely humored him, and now she was in a fine pickle. And though she had not promised to hire him if he passed, she would certainly seem churlish to refuse him the position.

Except she knew nothing about him.

Mouth turned down, and eyebrows pulled together, she ran a finger along the windowpane.

That was not precisely true.

She raised her head.

Lilly would write The University of Cambridge and make inquiries.

In the meanwhile, Zander could step in temporarily for Miss Sanders until Lilly either hired another viable candidate, or she verified he had told the truth.

He wanted the position.

Surely, that also meant he wanted to stay at Kelston Hall Children's Home.

An involuntary smile bent her mouth and her heart, the silly, stupid thing, fluttered.

She wanted him here too, and that might prove disastrous.

Naturally, she would need Charles's approval, but given the bond the men had already established, she would not be surprised if Charles did not perform a cartwheel or whoop with joy when she told him of her decision to employ Zander.

For the time being, in any event.

Lilly told herself hiring him was best for the children; and for the school too.

But the honest-to-God truth was, she did not want him to leave. She very much feared the stranger she had given her bed to might also have wiggled his way into her spinster's heart.

What she ought to do and what she wanted to do with that unforeseen conundrum were two vastly different things.

TWELVE

Kelston Hall's drawing room

That same evening after supper

The suspense nearly drove Zander mad.

Would Lilly hire him?

Charles had not remarked upon the subject, and Zander had been reluctant to pry, in case it appeared he was attempting to manipulate the situation.

Zander observed Lilly from beneath hooded eyes as she sat on the settee embroidering a handkerchief, as if his very future did not rely upon her decision to hire him.

When faced with the empty cavern that was his memory and hence his life, this place provided him with the security and peace he desperately craved. He would bite off his tongue before admitting it, but the truth was, he was scared.

He had no past, so he yearned for a future.

Lilly gave no hint in demeanor or expression regarding how he had scored on the examinations.

Earlier, he had been confident he had performed well, but little sprouts of doubt tried to rear their bothersome heads. Like weeds in a flower garden, he rooted them out, but the troublesome misgivings kept creeping back.

Never was a woman so impossible to read. She had mastered masking her emotions and, no doubt, through much practice had perfected the skill to a fine art.

Only when surprised did her soft brown eyes reveal her feelings. Then merely long enough for her to marshal her composure with the efficiency and discipline of a combat general in His Majesty's army before the bastions slammed closed.

A soft snore escaping him, Charles shifted in the armchair. His lanky legs stretched toward the hearth, his chin resting on his chest, and an open periodical laying in his lap, he dozed.

Zander canted his head and read the publication's title before crinkling his forehead into a dubious frown.

The Edinburgh Medical and Surgical Journal.

Poor chap.

Even in his off hours, he was ever the physician.

If the contents of the magazine had not put Charles to sleep, his late nights had likely caused his unintended nap. Perpetual violet circles rimmed his eyes beneath his spectacles, and he often yawned, mid-sentence.

According to Mrs. B, Charles rarely slept through the night.

For, though he was one of three doctors in the area, he was the only physician who did not demand coin for his fees but accepted items in trade. Hence, his services were in constant demand from the poorer residents, and the children's home regularly received interesting, if not useful, products.

Perhaps, it was his humble beginnings, Mrs. B. speculated, but Charles could not refuse to help anyone in need.

Upon further contemplation, that is likely where Lilly had acquired the hideous fabric for her gown.

After setting aside the travel book Zander had selected from the library earlier today, authored by Leonidas Westbrook—*why did that name seem familiar?*—Zander stood.

Lilly raised her gaze and regarded him for an extended moment with that unfathomable mien.

What went on in that brilliant mind of hers?

He could almost hear the cogs grinding and the wheels whirring.

The edges of her mouth quivered the merest bit when he nervously cleared his throat.

The minx.

She enjoyed his discomfort.

Not out of maliciousness.

Lilly did not have a malevolent bone in her body, nor was she one to toss her authority about like rose petals at a wedding.

Zander suspected her satisfaction arose from having made a logical decision, not a choice resulting from feminine sentiment.

With unhurried movements, she stored her embroidery threads in her sturdy sewing box and tucked the needle into a small embossed red leather needle case. Once she had stashed her embroidery supplies to her satisfaction, she glanced toward Charles, still sound asleep.

"Let's step outside, Zander, shall we?" she whispered as she swept across the room. "I do not wish to disturb Charles. The poor dear is in a constant state of exhaustion. What he needs is his own establishment in the village, but he will not consider leaving me to run the children's home on my own. He vows a man's presence keeps undesirables at bay."

There was some truth to that.

Zander joined her at the terrace door.

"Except, he is rarely around to assist, is he?" he murmured, daring to point out the fact.

She gave him a sharp, slightly startled, sideways glance. "True, but it is not from deliberate neglect."

Her soft tone held a thread of censure.

"I never meant to imply that it was." Zander opened the door for Lilly, and she swept past him and onto the small back terrace. "I only meant, he is a dedicated physician, despite the toll it takes on him physically and mentally."

"That he is." She gave a nod. "Even as a child, he was serious and solemn. When he committed to something, he always saw it through to the end. That dedication has not waned in adulthood."

An admirable trait.

Zander stared at the oak copse cast in twilight's shadows across the meadow. An obscure memory swirled around in his brain.

He rubbed his nose with two fingers. "Some doctors cannot handle the death and anguish. It destroys their spirit because they blame themselves for not saving every patient."

"You sound as if you know someone that happened to." Lilly leaned her left hip against the balustrade, her face slightly turned upward as she gazed across the landscape. "Do you?"

As always, she was straightforward—no mincing words.

From the corner of her eye, she considered him.

"I honestly do not know." He ran his palm along the smooth limestone balustrade.

At dusk, with the fading light of the day bathing her in gentle hues, she appeared lovely and feminine, despite the ugliness and severity of her gown. It did not escape Zander that the more time he spent with Lilly, the more attractive and desirable she became.

She glanced over at him.

"I have spoken with Charles, and he is in complete agreement." A sincere smile warmed her features as she extended her hand. "We would like to offer you the teaching position at Kelston Hall Children's Home, temporarily."

THIRTEEN

Kelston Hall's chilly, twilight terrace

Following a handful of stunned seconds

Zander nearly whooped in exhilaration, but dancing about the terrace might not be putting his best foot forward.

At once, he wrapped her hand in his palm, and his heart leaping for joy might not have been entirely due to excitement and relief.

Hoo'ooh. Hoo'ooh.

A stock dove's coo echoed from the oak copse.

A moment later, another answered.

Hoo'ooh. Hoo'ooh.

"Thank you, Lilly. You shall not regret it. I promise."

Reluctant to break the connection, he still held her hand.

A connection that went beyond her soft skin brushing against his calloused flesh.

A connection that both terrified and invigorated him.

The first star of the evening appeared in the sky. It winked at him from across the great expanse, almost as if to say, "You need not have fretted, foolish man."

"I would not make promises you may not be able to keep, Zander." A shadow passed over her features, and she withdrew her hand. "Remember, this arrangement is temporary."

Did she already have regrets?

Strangely bereft without her palm in his, Zander twined his fingers together behind his back. Doing so also kept him from turning her into his arms and kissing her until she was breathless and soft-kneed with desire.

A wicked fancy that had taken root several days ago and grew with intensity daily.

"Now that I am on the mend, is there somewhere else I can sleep so that you can have your bedchamber back?" His conscience would not allow him to continue to use her bed while she thrashed about on a hard floor.

"There are no beds available, but if Charles approves and says you are well enough, I shall see if we can find a place for a pallet."

A furrow appeared between her eyebrows, as it did when she was deep in thought.

"Perhaps, we can clear a section in the attic. The chimneys keep it warm, and you would have privacy." She gave him an apologetic smile. "It is not luxurious by any means. There are also mice and spiders up there."

In all honesty, Zander had thought he might have to sleep in the stables.

"That sounds perfect." Except for the bit about spiders. He loathed spiders.

It must have something to do with the monstrous spiders he had seen in Australia.

I have been to Australia.

Excitement ticked a staccato in his veins.

That must be a useful memory.

"I shall introduce you to the children tomorrow, and you can begin your duties next week." Lilly faced the meadow again. In the distance, the brook burbled sleepily. "I do not want you to overtax yourself too soon. We must decide on a surname for you too."

"Brook." The name jumped off his tongue as if it had been poised there, ready to be spoken. "I know you mentioned Field, but there is also a brook nearby."

"Indeed, there is." Her profile serene in the waning light, Lilly nodded. "It is called Hodgson Burn."

She pressed her lips together for an instant.

Something troubled her.

"Is there something else, Lilly?"

"I am writing Cambridge University. I hope that records are kept of First Class Honors and Second Wrangler recipients."

"Excellent idea."

And it was, so why was he not more excited about the prospect of discovering who he was?

Because once he did, his time here would be over.

"Lilly?"

He edged nearer until his thigh brushed the skirt of her gown.

This was utter insanity.

"You really should not address me by my given name. It is not proper and could lead to unwanted speculation." She angled her head to look at him, and her eyes widened at what she saw written on his face.

Undisguised desire.

For her.

"What...?"

She darted her tongue out to dampen her lower lip, and Zander nearly groaned out loud.

"Zander, why are you looking at me like that?"

"Because, my darling, I desperately want to kiss you."

"Oh." She blinked, pink tinting her rounded cheeks. "You do?"

She sounded so incredulous, it cleaved his heart.

"Very," he lowered his voice to a gravelly baritone, "*very* much."

Motionless, except for the gentle rise and fall of her chest, she stared at his mouth.

Encouraged, Zander lowered his head, inch by inch, fearful she might bolt and rob him of the sweet taste of her mouth.

"Do you want me to kiss you, Lilly?"

She flicked her gaze upward to collide with his for an instant before she averted her regard.

"I...I do. More than is prudent."

Thank God.

He edged lower still.

Just another couple of inches. Then, he would know bliss.

"But I cannot allow it, Zander," she said firmly, if somewhat breathlessly.

Ah, hell.

If he were not so disappointed, he would have admired her willpower, for her self-control far exceeded his.

Lilly braced her palm on his chest. "Haven't you considered that you might be married?"

Those softly murmured words cudgeled him.

Zander's breathing stalled.

Married?

No, I am not.

How could he be certain?

He did not feel married.

Would his heart yearn for Lilly if he loved another?

Not all marriages were love matches.

In fact, very few were.

Had he entered a marriage of convenience?

An arranged marriage?

Bollocks.

As usual, Lilly was correct.

As a man of honor, he could not kiss her unless he knew for certain that he was unentangled.

He lowered his forehead to rest against hers. "Are you always so sensible?"

"I fear so. To a fault sometimes. Regardless, it has served me well." She took two paces backward and faced him with courage he could not help but esteem. "If you want the position, nothing like this can ever happen again. If it does, Zander, I shall terminate you on the spot and send you packing at once."

"I understand." He did, but his bloody libido did not, and at this moment, the only thing that would calm his desire was an hour—*or four*—in the frigid brook.

"I would have your word, please." She folded her hands, once again, prim and proper.

By God, Lilly drove a hard bargain.

That she would take the word of a man she found nearly dead in her meadow and that she had once locked in her bedchamber for fear he was a criminal, struck Zander to his core.

He peered at her closely.

She trembled like a tender new leaf in a blustery wind.

For all her fortitude, Lilly appeared remarkably fragile at this moment. As if it took every last measure she possessed to keep her stalwart composure.

Did she need Zander to resist the temptation, this undefined attraction between them, because she was not positive she could?

That revelation buoyed his spirits, despite the disappointment thrumming through his veins.

Now was not the time.

Nevertheless, that did not mean another opportunity might not present itself, and by thunder, Zander would seize it. But only if he had verification that he was not married. This meant that until he knew his identity, the tempting woman before him was utterly off-limits.

"I give you my word as a gentleman that I shall not attempt to kiss you, Miss Lilibet Granger."

He winked and waggled his eyebrows to lighten the mood. "I shall not, however, refuse any overtures *you* make toward *me*."

She made an unladylike noise between a scoff and a snort.

Althelia does that too.

Who the blazes is Althelia?

"That shall happen when you catch lightning in a bottle *Mr. Brook*."

He burst out laughing.

"For you, Lilly, I would try. Even if it meant the death of me."

By God, Zander meant it, and that knowledge shook him to the soles of his borrowed shoes.

"Now you mock me." Hurt leeched into Lilly's voice.

"Never, sweet, Lilly."

Zander lifted her hand and brushed his lips across the knuckles. "Never."

Her face crumpled, and before she yanked her hand from his and turned and ran into the house, tears slipped from her eyes.

Why?

FOURTEEN

In the estate orchard

A sunny autumn afternoon six days later

A month.

An entire month.

Zander had been at Kelston Hall Children's Home for an entire month. Lilly could scarcely remember what life had been like before his arrival.

How could that be?

He fit in so well; it was as if he had always been here.

She really ought to sketch his image, now that he had completely healed from the brutal beating. Except, once the likenesses were passed around, someone would likely recognize him, and then he would go.

Out of her life forever.

That thought eviscerated her.

Things at Kelston Hall would return to the way they had been before Zander disrupted her orderly existence. Only, life would never be completely the same.

She had changed.

Zander meant much more to her than a mere stranger rescued from certain death or another capable instructor at the home.

More fool her for not promptly crushing the tender sentiments when they first sprouted, which she would have done forthwith, had she recognized her feelings for what they were.

That was the trouble with never having been infatuated, enamored, or in love before.

One did not know what had overcome one until it was too deuced late.

Still, she had determined to better control her emotions in the future. The night she had fled from him in tears still mortified her.

Stupid ninny.

When he had vowed that he would never mock her, something inside Lilly unfurled, and longings she had suppressed for years burst forth with such angst and yearning, she could not hold back her tears.

And she detested waterworks.

Useless, exasperating histrionics that until a week ago, she believed herself immune from.

Zander, dash him to ribbons, had proven her so very wrong.

Not so long ago, she had wanted him gone.

Now a vice squeezed her heart until she could not draw a breath whenever she imagined never seeing him again.

Despite her untenable fascination with him, Lilly remained a practical woman.

Of course, he would go.

What else would he do, for pity's sake?

Even if Zander could not remember precisely what it entailed, he had a life apart from Kelston Hall.

Women in her circumstances—*on the shelf spinsters*—illegitimate with a pockmarked face and a figure that ran toward plumpness, did not dare hope for anything more than a comfortable position to occupy their time until they became too aged to continue working.

Was she not already tremendously blessed?

Yes. Yes.

Of course, she was, *silly goose.*

For reasons known only to her, Miss Davenport had ensured Lilly a stable future.

So, why then, this past week since Zander said he wanted to kiss her—Lord, how Lilly wanted him to kiss her—had every waking moment been consumed with daydreams and woolgathering fantasies?

Wistful, fantastical notions that could never be, but she still yearned for with all of her being?

And the nights?

The nights were far worse.

She dreamed of Zander.

Heated, chaotic, tormentingly sensual visions, and in her scandalous dreams, Zander kissed her.

And...once upon a midnight dream...he had done more.

So much more.

Forbidden, wanton, unchaste things.

Heat scorched Lilly's cheeks, and she swiftly glanced around.

The unseasonably warm day brought a flush to the faces of many of the adults and children, picking fruit and gathering nuts.

Thank goodness.

She could blame her rosy complexion on the warm, late September afternoon and not the improper thoughts about the virile man a few feet away.

Much to her relief, the sheriff still had not called.

Lilly did not intend to contact him again, either.

Should Sheriff Wrottesley inquire why she had wanted to see him, she would mention the man she had recently seen twice, studying the house. Or at least he seemed to observe Kelston Hall.

In point of fact, he simply might be another newcomer to Prudhoe and wanted to familiarize himself with the area.

She had not mentioned the incidents to Charles or Zander. Nevertheless, a tiny worry rooted around in the back of her mind that, although highly unlikely, the loiterer could be connected to Zander's abduction.

Though her stomach turned and her lungs cramped at the pain he had endured, she could not regret the dire circumstances that had sent him to her doorstep.

Well, perhaps not on her doorstep, but onto Kelston Hall's lands.

Lilly likely would never have met him otherwise.

Children's laughter carried through the fresh, fragrant air as they scampered about the orchard and up and down ladders. Everyone in the household, except the stable boy and Mrs. B, busy cooking their supper, helped harvest the Golden Pippen and Ashmead's Kernal apples, Warden and Bergamot pears, and walnuts.

They would not harvest the quince until October, but in the meantime, cider and preserves must be made, fruit preserved, and walnuts dried for the winter.

Song thrushes, blackbirds, and robins chirped and bobbed among the laden branches, eager for the humans to depart so the birds could gorge themselves on fallen fruit too bruised to save.

Tonight, everyone would indulge in apple dumplings, served with cream, a tradition Lilly began several years ago as a reward for the children's and staff's hard work in harvesting the estate's bounty.

She loved this time of year, when the English countryside

blushed with the fiery golds and crimsons of autumn, and morning mist clung to the hillsides like a comforting blanket. The orchard brimmed with ripened fruit, and the cooler air made for cozy, shawl-wrapped walks beneath canopies of russet and amber as leaves crunched beneath her boots.

The hearth fires seemed more inviting and a cup of steaming tea or apple cider more calming, as the earth celebrated one last time in preparation for facing winter's starkness and harshness once again.

This year was even more special because of Zander's presence.

He had taken to teaching as if he had been instructing children for decades, rather than days. It was apparent from the worshipful looks the boys kept sending him, Zander had already made a mark upon the lads who needed a male mentor in their lives.

Charles, bless his kind heart, tried his best. However, given he was absent most days and did not interact with the children in the same capacity as an instructor, his relationship with the orphans was not as close.

Even the shyest girls slipped their little hands into Zander's, and Lilly had caught more than one female instructor ogling him like a French *Mille-feuille* or custard tart they would like to gobble up.

Drucilla Wobblecroft, five and fifty if she was a day, sidled next to Zander and batted her almost non-existent gray eyelashes. She added half a dozen apples to the already full basket he held, then coyly angled her head so that her hideous straw bonnet slid to the ground.

"Oh, dear," she murmured in mock dismay while pressing a hand to her ample bosom. "My bonnet has fallen."

Yes, that tends to happen when you untie the ribbons and then tilt your head.

Lilly made a mental note to have a conversation about

appropriate and acceptable behaviors with the female instructors as soon as possible. It would not do to have enamored teachers mooning about and perhaps, causing a scandal, because while she had worked hard to make the home self-sufficient, a handful of benevolent patrons regularly donated funds.

Still, she could not help but admire the way Zander's too-small shirt tightened across his broad back as he lifted a full produce basket onto the wagon before bending to retrieve the bonnet. Unlike Drucilla, however, Lilly covertly observed him from beneath her eyelashes, rather than openly gawking like an infatuated schoolgirl.

Just to ensure her secret was safe, however, she sent a swift glance around to see if anyone had noticed her appreciation. Everyone seemed engrossed in activities elsewhere, and she breathed a small sigh of relief.

Really, hiding her feelings became more difficult each day that Zander remained at Kelston Hall. As headmistress, she should set an example, not engage in the same untenable goggling of the home's only male instructor.

Not that she could blame the other teaching staff.

Plopping a fine specimen of masculinity in the middle of a bunch of spinsters was akin to tossing dry, brittle fodder on a toasty fire, and then pretending to be surprised when the blaze raged hotter.

Lilly ought to have foreseen the chaos hiring Zander would cause, but her secret feelings had blinded her.

True, she repeatedly told herself, she had hired him because doing so was practical, logical, wise, and prudent. However, when alone and forced to face the undeniable truth head-on, she must admit she had fairly jumped at the opportunity to keep him at Kelston Hall.

He brushed a leaf off the ratty atrocity that passed for a hat, then handed it to Miss Wobblecroft. "Here you are."

"Thank you *ever so* much, Mr. Brook," Miss Wobblecroft gushed, her chins folding into themselves and the mole with the black wiry hair near her mouth twitching with a life of its own. "What a pleasure to have a gentleman so close at hand."

She placed her plump hand on his rippling shoulder and tipped her mouth up into what could only be described as an improper invitation.

Lilly's stomach clenched tighter than a beggar's fist.

I am not jealous, she told herself sternly.

Her position as director demanded she nip this type of behavior in the bud at once.

That was all.

She had better have that conversation with the instructors as soon as possible.

"I do believe I am offended," Charles whispered in Lilly's ear. "Am I not also a gentleman?"

Lilly yelped in surprise, then playfully slapped his forearm in the manner a sister would an annoying younger brother.

"Do not sneak up on me, Charles. I nearly had an apoplexy."

Grinning, he winked. "If you had not been staring at Zander as if he were a licorice drop, you would have seen me approach."

FIFTEEN

After several humiliating heartbeats

"Do not be ridiculous, Charles. I was *not* staring," Lilly retorted with more emphasis than required.

You certainly were, too, staring.

A gentleman would not have mentioned her lapse in good judgment, but Charles was as near to a brother as she had, and they had pledged many years ago to always be honest and forthright with each other.

She dug her fingernails into her palms rather than remind him how often he sent longing looks toward Miss Charlene McKenzie, his senior by eight years, who seemed oblivious to Charles's warm regard.

"I was deciding what to do about Miss Wobblecroft," Lilly said beneath her breath while sending the mooning woman a pointed glance. She folded her arms. "She has become positively...predatory. For all we know, Zander is a married man. I cannot have the teachers making fools of themselves or acting like wantons."

"Wantons, *eh*?" Charles's voice shook with humor, but the thunderous look she leveled him brought his mirth under control.

"I am sure you will find a satisfactory solution, Lil."

Chastity belts?

Saltpeter?

Does saltpeter even work on women?

"I can prescribe nettle tea, willow bark, and camphor. They all cool the body's humors," he offered, helpfully, though he could not keep his face straight.

The rotter, teasing her so.

"A cold diet is thought to dampen sexual desire, but I am quite certain bloodletting is ineffectual for reducing libido." He chuckled at his poor jest.

Lilly ignored his ridiculous suggestions, for she suspected he directed them toward her and not the other teachers. That was what came of him being her best friend for most of their lives.

Charles took liberties that no one else dared, and Lilly rarely minded.

A chorus of, "Bunny. It's a bunny," from the youngest children interrupted their conversation.

Sure enough, a gray-brown rabbit pelted hell-bent for nothing toward the meadow, its little black-button eyes wide and terrified.

"I presume you need to speak with me, Charles?" Lilly said dryly as she continued picking apples.

Miss Wobblecroft still shadowed Zander's every move, and irritation tip-toed up Lilly's spine.

The woman was not paid to flirt.

Had she forgotten she had children to supervise?

Though to be fair, with the other teachers and servants present, it was not likely the boys and girls would get into much mischief. Unless Miles, George, and Joseph began lobbing apples at each other in an imitation of the Battle of Waterloo.

"I have to leave, Lil." Charles rubbed the back of his neck. "I just received a message that Mrs. Tillman is about to give birth to her eighth child, though the deed will likely be done before I arrive. It nearly was the last time. I shall probably have a goose or a couple of fat chickens for supper later in the week."

Mr. Tillman was a poulterer.

Lilly glanced around to take stock of the children, mentally counting them as had become a force of habit. She narrowed her eyes at a group of small girls, clustered together. "I shall have Mrs. B keep your supper warm. Or if you are not back tonight, have her lay out a tray of cold foods in the kitchen for when you return."

"Thank you." Charles patted her shoulder before hurrying away, but not, however, before he cast a swift, yearning glance at Miss McKenzie.

Did Miss McKenzie have any idea Charles held a *tendre* for her?

It was not Lilly's place to interfere.

Besides, a relationship between the two was forbidden as long as Charlene worked at Kelston Hall, which was probably why she never glanced twice in Charles's direction. Like many women alone in the world, the only thing between Charlene McKenzie and the street was her position. She would not risk losing it—not even for a chance at love.

Lilly knew that feeling.

Suppressing a sigh, she returned her attention to the little girls.

What were they up to?

"Miss Wobblecroft?" she said.

No response.

Slightly exasperated, Lilly repeated, a trifle louder and firmer, "*Miss. Wobblecroft?*"

Miss Wobblecroft dragged her infatuated regard from Zander and blinked several times at Lilly as if she could not quite focus.

Zander met Lilly's gaze over Miss Wobblecroft's head.

Hilarity glimmered in his eye.

"*Mmm?* Yes?" Miss Wobblecroft slid Zander a sideways glance. "Did you need something, Miss Granger?"

Obviously.

"Please see what has captured the youngest girls' fascination." Lilly directed her attention to a circle of six squatting girls, including Nellie Picket, staring at something between them. Nellie possessed an insatiable curiosity and a penchant for unintentionally getting into mischief. "Wasps are gorging themselves on the fallen fruit. We do not want anyone to get stung."

"Oh, indeed. We cannot have that." Miss Wobblecroft plopped her bonnet on her head and, with one last libidinous glance at Zander's chest, made haste toward the captivated girls.

"Gir-rls? Gir-rls?" she called, in a sing-song voice, breaking the word into two syllables. She quickened her pace, causing her hat to bounce like a toy boat upon a pond. "Nellie, Marsha, Annie, Flora, Alice, Cora! Away from there this instant."

She made shooing motions with her hands as she huffed and puffed her way toward the fascinated girls.

"Thank you." Amusement creased the corner of Zander's good eye and twisted his firm mouth upward.

Deciding to pretend ignorance, Lilly raised her nose. "Whatever for?"

He chuckled and swiped a hand across his moist forehead.

"Come now, Lilly. You have always been straightforward with me." He jerked his chin toward Miss Wobblecroft's departing form. "You saved me from Miss Wobblecroft's clumsy attempts at flirting."

It did not help that he had rolled his shirtsleeves to his elbows, exposing sable-covered forearms, or that he had forgone a neckcloth and a delightful vee of manly throat and curly jet-black chest hair peeked from his shirt every time he moved. And it was positively indecent the way his too-small trousers showed off his muscular legs.

"Yes, well, I intend to have a word with all the female staff. Decorum must prevail." Lilly pressed her lips together. "I shall remind them what happened to Miss Sanders for failing to adhere to the conduct codes she signed. Just because we have an attractive man in our midst does not mean they can throw discretion to the wind."

"*Attractive man?*" A pleased grin split his face.

Blast and bother.

Lilly had not meant to say that out loud.

Now Zander would be utterly impossible.

He bent his head and whispered, "What about you?"

Good Lord.

Of all the gall.

Was he asking if she thought him handsome?

The brazen cad, fishing for compliments.

"I..." She choked on her response, but after closing her eyes for three seconds and dredging up her equanimity, managed in a calm voice to ask, "What do you mean, what about me?"

His nearness discombobulated her.

"Did you sign a code of conduct too, Lilly?"

Of course, she had.

When she was a teacher under Mrs. Reubins's authority.

But—darn the oversight—she had forgotten to have Zander sign a code of conduct. She would remedy that today, by Jove.

"You are not going to bait me, Zander Brooks." After dropping four more greenish-yellow apples into the bushel basket, she squinted at him. "Tomorrow, we are going to the village and ordering you new clothing."

Clothes that fit and do not practically beg women to lust after you.

He quirked an eyebrow, the glint in his gray eye indecipherable.

"Did you mean to say that aloud, Lilly?"

SIXTEEN

Still in the orchard. Still Sunny. Still afternoon

Ten hilarious heartbeats later

Zander could not contain his broad grin as he awaited Lilly's reply. If he was not an incorrigible cad, he would have ignored her, speaking her thoughts aloud.

But what was the fun in that?

Besides, his masculine pride swelled at her accidental admission, and when she was as flustered as she was now, she was quite adorable. Even in the atrocious dowdy brown gown, she had probably donned for the outdoor work.

Regardless, try as she might to appear like a drab wren or a dull pipit, Lilibet Granger was much more like a starling or grackle with breathtaking, iridescent colors shining forth in the right light.

One just had to be observant and look for her hidden beauty.

Just now, Lilly gaped at him, wholly horrified, for a half

dozen seconds before slapping her hand across her mouth and shaking her head.

Leaning nearer and savoring her delicate fragrance, Zander whispered for her ears alone, "Do not fret. I shall not tell anyone you lust after me."

Her brown eyes grew rounder and rounder and then sparks lit the irises as ire replaced her shock and embarrassment.

"I do not!" She poked a finger at his chest.

Hard.

Ouch.

That would leave a bruise, for certain. He rubbed the offended spot.

"You egotistical dunderhead," she snapped with more fire than Zander had ever witnessed in her before. "I most assuredly am too sensible to lu—do any such irrational thing."

What a delightful, adorable prude.

Zander almost snorted because she refused to say the word *lust* again, but as riled as she had become, she might haul off and slap him. Most especially if he reminded her that lust did not listen to reason or logic, which is what made it such a dangerous, unpredictable beast.

"But not all of my staff possesses the same degree of pragmatism, and it is my responsibility to ensure they do not make choices or behave in a manner that will in any way bring censure upon Kelston Hall Children's Home," she finished on a breathless rush.

"I apologize, Lilly." He touched her shoulder. "I would never—"

"Miss Granger?" Miss McKenzie called.

Just as well she had interrupted him before he made an asinine declaration Lilly would not want to hear and he had no business professing.

"We are done picking the fruit, so we're taking the children to the house to clean up now." With a nod, Miss McKenzie indicated Miss Wobblecroft and Mrs. Ruth Jones, both of whom practically leered at him.

"We are going too, Miss Granger." The maid, Florence, gave a little bob and a wave. "Mrs. B will need our help with the apple dumplings."

She and the other two maids, sisters Martha and Eliza, walked side by side toward the main house.

"Very good. I shall be up shortly." Forehead puzzled, Lilly glanced around. "I did not realize how quickly the fruit and nuts had been gathered."

Not only was the wagon beside Zander and Lilly filled with baskets, but several more clusters of bushel baskets sat throughout the orchard. The abundant harvest was a blessing for the home and would ensure plenty of fruit preserves, tarts, and the like throughout the long winter months.

Zander planned to be here to enjoy them as well, but who knew what his future held?

Charles still maintained Zander's memory could come flooding back at any moment. The minutest thing might trigger a recollection and open the floodgates. Then there was the letter Lilly had written to Cambridge, which might very well help identify him.

Never had Zander been so conflicted.

If he discovered who he was, then he would know if he was unmarried and free to pursue his growing feelings for Lilly. Or if he had already exchanged vows with another and must do right by his wife. Not to mention trying to wade through the nefarious circumstances that had brought him to Kelston Hall to begin with.

He still believed he had been abducted, and that meant someone posed a threat and danger to him and possibly to Lilly and the others because of his presence here. That knowledge plagued him and kept him awake long after the house had settled each night.

Zander should leave.

That would be the unselfish thing to do.

The noble and honorable thing.

For the safety and wellbeing of everyone at Kelston Hall.

But he had discovered he was a selfish arse.

Not only did he have nowhere to go, he refused to leave Lilly unless forced to. She might never know the depths of his feelings for her, but he would protect her with his life.

Regardless, there was something to the adage that ignorance was bliss because at present, not knowing who he was, if he was married, or who had abducted and beaten him, meant he could continue this happy interlude.

And he was happy.

Very much so, truth be told.

Despite all those irksome uncertainties.

He gave a mental shrug.

"I shall drive the wagon to the root cellar entrance," he offered, by way of apology.

Zander should not tease Lilly so.

She was not accustomed to banter and jesting unless it came from Charles.

"I can do it," she demurred with a stubborn jut of her chin. "I always do, unless Charles is here."

Which was hardly ever, no doubt, through no fault of his.

"I am certain you can, but there is no shame in accepting help when it is offered." Zander extended his hand to assist her onto the seat.

After a moment's hesitation, she placed her palm in his and agilely climbed onto the driver's seat.

Closing his fist to capture the feeling of touching her and the unexpected jolt of awareness that thrummed through him at the contact, he marched to the other side and jumped aboard.

Only the rhythmic creak of the wooden wagon wheels and the soft clip-clop of the horse's hooves interrupted the silence as they approached the grand house. The sun bathed the stones in a warm glow and cast golden light on the rolling green hills.

"What would you never?" Lilly turned halfway to gaze at him, her silly, oversized hat brim flopping low on her forehead.

Zander quirked an eyebrow. "Would I never...?"

"Before Miss McKenzie interrupted, you said that you would never..." More than curiosity brimmed in her big brown eyes.

He inhaled a lungful of air and held it for a few seconds before releasing his breath. "I was about to make another vow, but given your less-than-enthusiastic response the other night, it is probably just as well I did not finish."

Hands folded in her lap, the nails slightly dirty from her afternoon of harvesting, she regarded him, serious and grave. "That is probably wise. Just as you cannot unring the church bell or catch smoke that has left the chimney, words cannot be unspoken. Sometimes it is better that they not be said at all."

He dared to place his hand over hers and give her fingers a small squeeze.

"Someday, I hope I have the chance to speak freely, Lilly. When we both know who I am."

A fragile, sad smile bent her mouth, but she merely nodded.

"Tell me, if you will," he said to break the solemn, oppressive mantle that seemed to have settled over them, "how did you and Charles come to own Kelston Hall?"

At once, her countenance brightened. "It is rather a long, intriguing story."

"I would still like to hear it." And Zander did.

He wanted to know everything about Lilly.

Her features softened as she looked over the horse's head. "The abbreviated version is that when Viscount Merrivale fell upon hard times, he sold the house to his spinster sister, Matilda Davenport."

Davenport. Davenport.

That name rang a bell.

Where did Zander know it from?

Bollocks, this lack of memory had become a deuced nuisance.

Oblivious to his frustration, Lilly unfolded, then refolded her hands.

"She turned the manor into a children's home and oversaw its operation from a distance until her death. I was sent here as a toddler, soon after the home opened. Charles came along a short while later. As the youngest children here, we became like siblings. We even shared a room for the first few years."

"It is obvious you are very close." Zander glanced over at her. "Your eyes are a similar color."

She laughed.

"That is where the resemblance ends. He is tall and thin, and I am..." She gestured toward her voluptuous figure. "Neither."

"You are lovely, Lilly."

A becoming blush crept up her cheeks, and she cleared her throat before continuing her tale.

"Miss Davenport visited the home regularly, bringing gifts for all the children when she came, but she always had something special for Charles and me.

"The former headmistress thought Miss Davenport doted on us because we were the youngest children, and she had no children of her own.

"She never knew that Mrs. Reubins took our treats from

us the moment Miss Davenport left. Mrs. Reubins said it was not fair to the other children."

Lilly's voice hardened and took on a tone Zander had never heard before at the mention of the former headmistress.

"I take it you were not overly fond of Mrs. Reubins?" He shot her a sideways glance, trying to read her expression.

Her hideous hat made it impossible.

Lilly shook her head.

"She was an awful, cruel, vindictive person who should never have been allowed around children, much less in charge of a children's home.

"She threw a conniption fit when Miss Davenport insisted that I be hired as an instructor when I was sixteen. Mrs. Reubins had an even greater tizzy when Miss Davenport paid for Charles to go to university and medical school."

Why would an aristocrat go to such efforts for two orphans?

"Miss Davenport sounds like an extraordinary woman." He flicked the reins.

A bothersome suspicion took root.

"Why do you think she favored you and Charles?" Zander asked.

A frown turned Lilly's mouth downward.

"That is a question we have both asked many, many times, to which we still have no answer.

"Not that Charles and I are not eternally grateful.

"Only God knows where we would be if it weren't for her benevolence." She peeked at him, her eyes bright with appreciation. "She left us what remained of her fortune too, with the stipulation we use it to operate the school."

Zander gave a low whistle and shook his head. "Honestly, I am surprised Viscount Merrivale did not object, especially since he was pockets to let."

Surprise skittered across Lilly's features.

"I had not considered that, but it was her money to do with as she pleased. She told me so herself when I was about fourteen.

"She had inherited a tidy sum from her mother who had inherited from her mother. They invested and increased their fortunes, which aggravated their menfolk to no end."

Bravo for them.

Lilly chuckled, a sultry echo of amusement. "She made it clear that it delighted her to no end that the men in their lives could not touch a penny of their money."

Zander pondered that information for a minute.

He would wager it infuriated the Davenport men when she bequeathed her wealth to a small, countryside children's home. Miss Davenport's will must have been ironclad, or else her male relatives would have already taken the matter to court and claimed her funds.

Tenderness softened the corners of Lilly's eyes, and she spread her palms wide on her thighs.

"She always smelled of lilacs and was infallibly kind to me.

"It was a shame she never had children.

"She was pretty, and with her fortune and lineage, I would have thought men would have been eager to wed her, even if she did have a few barely noticeable pockmarks beneath her artfully applied rice powder."

Zander snapped his head up.

Pockmarks?

Coincidence?

Mayhap. There were still occasional outbreaks. But not bloody likely.

By thunder, if and when, he regained his memory, he meant to look into the matter.

He would not say a word to Lilly in the meantime.

Could Lilly be the late Matilda Davenport's illegitimate daughter?

It certainly would explain a lot.

SEVENTEEN

In Kelton Hall's main corridor on the way to Lilly's office

The middle of October—shortly after the midday meal

Would the *letter* be here today?

The correspondence from the University of Cambridge that Lilly had eagerly awaited, yet simultaneously dreaded?

Those questions had become a daily ritual for her, and each day her stomach twisted into a glob of anxiety when she checked the post.

The fabric of her new mazarine blue wool gown swished softly as she proceeded down the corridor, lost in thought.

Mouth drawn into a tight line of expectancy, she thumbed through the correspondences she collected from the half-table in the entry that had been delivered while she ate luncheon with Zander and Mrs. Jones.

Miss Wobblecroft and Miss McKenzie supervised the children while they ate in what had once been the grand ballroom.

The four instructors rotated supervising the students' dining.

Lilly turned over a creamy rectangle—foolscap folded into a tidy envelope.

The postmark caught her eye.

Cambridge.

It came.

Her heart catapulted to her throat and then plummeted to her feet, where it flopped around like a bass tossed upon the riverbank at Thamesmead.

She flushed hot, then cold, then hot again.

How could a mere correspondence cause such consternation?

Because this letter could change everything.

It might reveal Zander's identity.

And then...then he would leave.

Lilly did not doubt that truth.

Her heartbeat quickened with fear.

Or was it anticipation?

She honestly was uncertain which, but the letter's arrival had thrown her into a proper pucker.

After another two weeks of Zander's company, she could no longer deny the truth; she had stupidly fallen in love with him.

Fool. Fool. Fool.

She had not even been aware of what was happening until it was too late, and he had completely taken possession of her heart.

Like a naïve schoolgirl, Lilly had become enamored of the first man to toss a rakish smile her way and wear her defenses down with kindness and charm. Naturally, she did not count Charles among those men.

He was, in every way but blood, her brother.

Placing her thumbnail on the red wax seal, she bit her lower lip as she cast a furtive glance up and down the corridor.

No.

Not here.

Despite the almost overwhelming urge to tear the letter open and scour the contents, Lilly would wait until she was alone, when no one could witness her reaction to whatever news—welcome or dreaded—the small rectangle held.

A crash followed by a loud thump and the distinct sound of glass breaking made Lilly jerk her head up.

A child's shrill cry rang out immediately.

Her blood froze in her veins.

What in heaven's name?

Lifting her skirts, she rushed toward the source of the commotion. She hurtled into the dining room but stopped short at the scene before her.

Eddy Cartwright lay on the floor, a hunk of cheese in one little hand and a fistful of salted beef in the other. What once had been pale cream ceramic dishes, along with glass tumblers, lay shattered around him.

She tossed the correspondence on the table.

Mrs. B and Florence tore through the kitchen door just as Lilly reached the weeping child and fell to her knees beside him.

Zander and Miss McKenzie trotted in behind her.

"Oh dear." As if she had sprinted to the dining room, Miss McKenzie's breath came in gulps.

She likely had.

"I wondered where the little mite had got himself off to." Concern pleated the corners of her eyes. "I have been searching everywhere for him."

Life as a street urchin had taught Eddy the art of hiding well.

Lilly gathered the sobbing child, still clutching the food, into her arms.

"Eddy, darling whatever were you doing?"

"Saving food for later," Eddy mumbled into her neck.

Her heart wrenched.

"I did not steal it," he rushed to assure her. "It was left on the table."

It was not the first time Eddy had sneaked away to horde food.

Orphaned and wandering the streets of Corbridge for God only knew how long, Eddy had not completely adjusted to his life at Kelston Hall. The newest child here, the troubled lad still feared he would not have enough to eat.

The Reverend Thomas Fenton had brought the starving little boy to Kelston Hall just before Zander had been found in the meadow. Living on a stipend, and with six children of his own, the man of God could not afford to take Eddy himself.

Reverend Fenton did not know Eddy's age, and neither did the boy.

From examining the lad's teeth, Charles estimated Eddy to be between six and eight years old, but because of malnourishment, he was extremely small for his age. One could easily mistake him for a five-year-old except for the unnatural maturity in his grave gaze.

More should be done for unfortunate waifs like Eddy. Lilly could not comprehend the lack of provision for the urchins and it frustrated her.

Nor could she have turned the big, blue, sad-eyed child away, even if it meant cramming another bed into an already crowded bedchamber. Not for the first time, she wished the children's home were bigger and she could accommodate more needy boys and girls.

But she was a realist.

That would require more funds than she could afford. It was better to operate Kelston Hall efficiently and make certain the children already here were provided for than entertain grand schemes and risk losing everything.

Then where would the other children at Kelston Hall be?

On the streets, as Eddy had been.

That was a horrific existence, and most children did not survive long.

Still, that had not kept Lilly from sketching her dream home, which could house upward of one hundred children. She hid the drawing in her desk and, once in a while, would drag it out and consider *what if...?*

What was life without hopes and dreams?

Even for a long on-the-shelf, plump, pockmarked spinster.

Nevertheless, Lilly's pragmatic side, more often than not, scoffed at such drivel.

Living with one's head in the clouds could only lead to disappointment and heartache. She had repeated that mantra too many times to count.

At times, the monologue helped center her again, and at others, the inarguable truth filled her with despondency.

Zander crouched beside her and gently lifted a shock of Eddy's midnight hair away.

"He is bleeding, Lilly."

Bending her neck, she noticed the blood she had missed in her haste to comfort the boy.

Eddy bore a cut across his forehead and three scarlet ribbons ran down the child's damp face.

"I do not think he will need stitches, though." Zander folded his new handkerchief and pressed it to Eddy's brow.

Lilly hid a wince.

They would never get the bloodstains out of the cloth.

"I shall get the medicine chest." Mrs. B disappeared back into the kitchen while Florence began clearing the rest of the table.

Lilly continued to cuddle the child, who had stopped crying but still clung to her. Charles was not at Kelston Hall, and she did not know when he would return. That meant she would have to care for the little chap.

It certainly was not the first time, nor would it be the last.

"I shall let Miss Wobblecroft and Mrs. Jones know where Eddy is." Miss McKenzie offered a sympathetic smile. "The students are off for a nature walk this afternoon if he feels up to it."

Perking up, Eddy lifted his head.

"Will we see beetles and snails and frogs and maybe even a snake, Miss McKenzie?"

Excitement laced the boy's voice at the thought.

"We very well may." To her credit, Miss McKenzie, who loathed creepy crawlies of any kind, nodded and pasted an enthusiastic smile on her face. "The weather is still mild, so if we are truly fortunate, perhaps a bee-fly, or if we are very lucky, even a hummingbird hawk-moth. Wouldn't that be grand?"

Eddy gave a fervent nod.

"Hold still, young man," Zander ordered good-naturedly. "I am trying to staunch the flow of blood."

"We shall be on the terrace shortly. Join us if you feel up to it, Eddy."

Miss McKenzie crossed to the entrance. Glancing over her shoulder, she swung her too shrewd gaze between Lilly and Zander, as if to say, *Exactly what is going on between the two of you?*

EIGHTEEN

A quarter after two that same day

Just perfect.

All Lilly needed was the staff speculating about her and Zander after her recent lecture about acceptable and appropriate behavior regarding him.

"Eddy, I need to put you on the table, so I can look at your cut."

Preparing to stand, Lilly shifted the child. He weighed little, but resting on her knees made rising while holding him difficult.

"Eddy, hold my handkerchief to your head," Zander said.

After switching the salted beef to his other hand, still gripping the cheese, the child complied.

Zander scooped him into his arms as easily as if he had lifted a puppy and rose with enviable animalistic grace.

Lilly observed him from beneath her lashes as he lowered

Eddy onto the table. In his new black trousers, navy frock coat, and navy and black striped waistcoat, Zander looked every bit the dashing rogue, and her tummy fluttered in appreciation.

Ninny.

Goose cap.

Dolt.

Numpty.

Their shopping expedition had not only resulted in him acquiring new clothing, but she had indulged in two ready-made gowns for herself; the wool creation she wore today and a stunning currant-red silk.

The latter was a divine creation meant for formal occasions, and she still did not know why she had purchased it. Except, the look in Zander's eye when he saw her in it made her feel positively ravishing.

Lilly had purchased the gowns at bargain prices too, because the woman they had been commissioned for left town without paying for them. She, too, possessed a fuller figure, and the seamstress needed only to take in the waist for the gowns to fit like they had been custom-made for Lilly.

Grateful not to be stuck with gowns she might not sell, the seamstress had not charged Lilly for the alterations.

"Do not move, young man. I do not want you to fall again," Zander ordered with a wink before he turned to extend a hand to help Lilly stand.

She slipped her palm into his, and a squishy sensation enveloped her.

Oh, this was getting utterly ridiculous.

Soon she would dissolve into a puddle at his feet.

Zander tightened his grip the merest bit.

Had he felt the sensation too?

She cleared her throat to dispel her frayed nerves and to break the sexual tension as thick as custard in the room.

"Let me have the food, Eddy," Lilly said. "I shall set it aside for you, while I clean your cut."

His eyes grew wide and wary.

She gently cupped his chin and peered into his anxious eyes. Eyes far too wise and jaded for his tender years.

"I promise, you will never go hungry here, Eddy. Never. Do you trust me?"

He gave a solemn nod and released his death grip on the meat and cheese.

Mrs. B appeared with the medicine chest, atop which sat a plate of ginger biscuits.

Only a step behind her, Martha carried a basin of water, a brush, and a dustpan. After placing the basin on the table, Martha squatted and swept up broken ceramic shards.

"I always prescribe a biscuit or two for situations like this. I vow they truly speed the healing process." Mrs. B winked at Eddy before turning away to return to her domain.

Bless her.

Eddy's face lit up, and he darted his small tongue to the corner of his mouth.

"I brought a few extras, Mr. Brook," Mrs. B tossed over her shoulder, as flirtatious as any demimonde. "I know how fond you are of sweets."

Lilly almost rolled her eyes.

Really, must Mrs. B be so blatant?

Zander grinned and waggled his eyebrows. "Nothing is as sweet as you, dear lady."

Oh, for the love of God.

Lilly did roll her eyes then.

What an unrepentant scallywag.

Mrs. B cackled with delight before her expression grew graver. "Miss Granger, a lad from the village brought a note 'round a while ago. My sister-in-law is ailing. Might I spend the afternoon and night with her? I shall cook supper before I leave."

"Of course you can." Lilly cast her a smile. "Please give her my regards and take her a basket of food too."

"I shall, and thank you." Untying her apron, Mrs. B disappeared into the kitchen.

"Can I have a biscuit?" Eddy asked, never taking his attention off the plate.

"You may have a treat after I wash the blood away. You need to hold very still," Lilly admonished softly as she dipped a cloth into the warm water. "Can you pretend to be a soldier in His Majesty's Army and do that for me?"

"Yes." Eddy gazed at her with such trust that a lump of emotion clogged her throat.

He and all the other children were why she did this.

Why she had never seriously considered marrying, not that she had ever had a suitor.

Who would look after the orphans if she left?

Love them like she did?

Folding his arms, the fabric pulling taut over his biceps, Zander rested his lean hip against the table and unabashedly stared at Lilly as she tended to Eddy.

What was he thinking?

She ought to tell him to stop gawping before a maid noticed and misinterpreted his interest; but chastising him now would only draw unwanted attention.

As Lilly cared for the child, Florence headed toward the kitchen, carefully balancing dishes in her arms. Having collected the larger broken pieces, Martha swept up the last of the remnants of the dishes and glasses.

"Thank you, Florence and Martha." Lilly smiled at the maids.

They smiled in return before dipping half curtsies and disappearing into the kitchen.

Lilly finished cleaning Eddy's cut and covered the wound with beeswax and comfrey ointment to protect it from infection.

"I do not think you need a bandage, Eddy." She glanced at Zander, still studying her with unnerving intensity. "What do you think, Mr. Brook?"

A half-smile cocked his mouth up on one side.

He leaned close—too close.

Lilly inhaled his musky manly scent, and her stomach did that strange thing it did when she was near to him.

Florence returned to gather more dishes, and Zander retreated to a respectable distance.

"I agree." Nodding, he ruffled the boy's raven hair. "But you must take care not to touch or bump the cut, lad. You do not want to contaminate it or cause it to start bleeding again."

"Yes, Mr. Brook." Eddy nodded and eyed the ginger biscuits longingly. "Can I have a biscuit now?"

"You may have two for being such a brave soldier." Lilly passed him two biscuits. "Do you feel up for the nature walk, Eddy?"

Chewing happily, he nodded again. "Yes. I want to find a snake."

"Go along with you, then." Lilly kissed the crown of his head. "Florence, will you please escort Eddy to the terrace to join the others? Make sure he wears his coat and cap."

"Yes, Miss Granger." Florence extended her hand and wiggled her fingers. "Come along, Eddy."

Without a jot of hesitation, Eddy entwined his small fingers with hers.

Lilly bent her mouth into a pleased smile.

He *was* adjusting and would continue to do so.

She just had to keep reassuring him.

A month ago, he would not have trusted Florence enough to hold her hand.

After they had gone, Zander gently touched Lilly's cheek as she put away the medical supplies.

"You would make a wonderful mother, Lilly."

His gesture and words so startled her, she fumbled with the lid to the ointment, nearly dropping it.

"Do you ever long for your own children?" he asked.

NINETEEN

After a handful of embarrassing seconds

Though her fingers had grown clumsy and pickle-sized, Lilly finally managed to place the lid on the ointment tin.

With a mere glance, Zander threw her into a dither.

Of course, she wanted children, but she had determined years ago it was not her lot in life.

"I have dedicated my life to the children at Kelston Hall, Zander." She placed the tin in the medicine chest and then gave him a sideways glance.

"What about you? Do you want children?"

Dash it to ribbons.

At her folly, she almost groaned aloud.

He might already have children.

The thought sat like curdled milk in her stomach. Not that he might have children, but what it meant if he had a family.

If he did, they must be worried sick about him.

"I have always liked children." A skillful deflection.

He leaned over and snatched three biscuits off the plate. As he bit into the crisp, spicy sweetness, his attention fell on the correspondence Lilly had tossed onto the table in her haste to reach Eddy.

Slowly straightening, Zander lifted the top letter.

"From Cambridge," he muttered beneath his breath, a hint of something Lilly could not identify, rendering his voice husky.

He glanced between Lilly and the rectangle he held between his thumb and forefinger.

"I was on my way to my office to open it, when I heard Eddy's cry." Why Lilly felt the need to explain herself mystified her.

Zander nodded but remained silent.

Could he be as concerned as she was?

"I fully intend to share the contents with you, Zander."

She swiped a tendril of hair that had come loose away from her face.

And there she went again.

Her tongue seemed to have taken on a life of its own and jabbered away without her permission. A most disturbing development, and one she must put an end to at once.

Was he as worried as Lilly that whatever was written on that paper would send their worlds upon their heads?

That they had no more control over what happened next than they did the sun rising and setting on the horizon each day?

Zander dropped the letter, and then the cookies onto the table.

Before Lilly knew what he was about, he gathered her into his arms and drew her against his hard chest.

His lips hovered above hers.

"That letter may well tumble us tail over top. So, before you open it and everything changes, I want to kiss you, Lilly."

He grazed a finger over her cheek, the contours and planes of his beloved face taut with suppressed desire.

"Will you let me, Lilly? Let us share this one moment? Mayhap, the only one we shall ever have?"

She should say no and pull away from his embrace.

It is what an upright, moral woman would do without hesitation. Without regret or recrimination.

What Lilly should do and what she wanted to do wrestled for domination, but the outcome was predetermined.

Because Zander was right.

The contents of the letter would likely leave her floundering in a jumble and, by all that was holy, at least she would have his splendid kiss to remember him.

For the kiss *would be* splendid. Spectacular. Glorious.

How could it not?

"Yes, Zander."

Was that breathless, sultry voice hers?

"Kiss me."

Still in the dining room

A SATISFIED GROAN throttled its way up Zander's throat as he captured Lilly's mouth in a searing kiss. He honestly did not know what he would have done if she had refused.

The joining of his and Lilly's mouths was everything he had dreamed it would be and more.

So much more.

His pent-up desire threatened to ignite them into a blazing conflagration. And by God, he would willingly burn to cinders for the opportunity to hold her and taste her mouth. To say with his caresses and lips what he dared not voice.

Lord, was there ever such a magnificent woman?

She had become so beautiful and cherished to him; he hardly noticed the light smattering of pox scars on her face.

Though it was unwise, and someone could interrupt them at any moment, he pressed her nearer, one hand between her shoulder blades, and the other at the small of her back.

Twining her arms around his neck, she molded her soft, sweet lips and luscious body to his, giving as much as she took. Though obviously a novice at kissing, she eagerly explored his mouth, mimicking his movements. Her little sighs as she pressed into him almost drove him over the edge—past the point of retreat.

Somewhere in the house, a longcase clock chimed twice.

Careful. Caution.

This was madness.

He must stop.

For Lilly's sake and his.

Dredging up every ounce of his self-control, Zander lifted his mouth from hers and set her away from him.

Her lips, moist and full, glowed cherry-red from his fervent kisses.

She appeared so ravishing and alluring, so muddled and bemused that he fisted his hands to keep from hauling her back into his arms and finishing what he had started—to hell with decorum and the servants' delicate sensibilities.

But Zander was a gentleman.

He might not know his name or where he came from, but at his core, he knew he was an honorable man.

More importantly, Lilly was a lady, and he would not treat

her like a dockside harlot and take her upon the dining room table.

Imagine the scandal.

Her eyes wide and still slightly dazed, Lilly put two shaky fingers to her lips.

With a single glance, anyone with an iota of common sense would comprehend what had occurred between them.

"I...I did not know a kiss could be like that," Lilly whispered, dazed.

Most kisses are not, darling.

Unrepentant masculine pride roared through Zander's veins.

Out of sheer preservation against giving into his baser instincts, he tore his gaze from her and picked up the letter. "Shall we see what it says?"

Shifting her befuddled attention to the small rectangle, she gave a reluctant nod, the lock of blonde hair bouncing near her temple. "In my office, though."

Because she wanted to protect his privacy, or because she did not want to chance a servant seeing her response? As stalwart as she had shown herself to be these past weeks, Zander still suspected the latter.

They strode in silence to her office.

Was she reliving their torrid kiss? For he sure the hell was.

Shoulders squared, chin up, she marched slightly ahead of him.

Why did it feel as though this was a march to the gallows?

Despite the somberness of the moment, Zander could not help but admire her composure and strength.

And the marvelous sway of her plump derriere.

A delectable derriere he yearned to smooth his hands over, preferably sans her clothing.

You are a hopeless libertine.

Part of Zander wanted to seize the letter and toss it into

the fire, and another part could not wait to see what it said. He may not remember who he was, or if he was married, but by God, he absolutely knew that never had a woman had him at such sixes and sevens before.

Once inside Lilly's office, she closed the door.

Rather than sit behind her desk, she sank onto the oak framed settee, covered in dark blue worsted wool.

She gestured to a nearby armchair.

"Please, make yourself comfortable, Zander."

She had never taken on airs with him or any of the other staff.

Just another thing to raise her in his esteem.

Zander took a position near the unlit fireplace. Though the middle of October, to save on fuel, Lilly only permitted fires lit in occupied rooms.

Her diligent management and economizing ensured the continuation of the children's home. Many formally trained men could not attain and maintain what she had. That spoke to her intellect, entrepreneurial spirit, and keen insight and perception.

"No, thank you." He clasped his hands behind his back. "If you do not object, I would rather stand."

"Not at all." She cracked the seal and swiftly scanned the letter.

Did her shoulders slump the merest bit?

Clenching his teeth and clasping his hands until they grew numb, he braced himself for the worst.

"What does it say, Lilly?" he asked softly, taking care to keep any alarm or concern from his tone.

"Here. Read it for yourself." She passed the less-than-crisp, travel-worn paper to Zander.

·   ·   ·

THE REGISTRAR'S Office of Cambridge University regrets to inform you

that, without the specific year of reference, it is not possible to definitively

identify which former students were awarded First Class Honors or held

the title of Second Wrangler. Our records are meticulously kept and

organized by academic year, and the distinctions of First Class Honors and

Second Wrangler are conferred annually to multiple students. Therefore, to

provide accurate information, we kindly request the relevant year or

additional details pertaining to the period in question.

"NOT PARTICULARLY HELPFUL, IS IT?" Zander lifted his regard to meet her troubled gaze as he refolded the letter and passed it back to her.

Relief sluiced through him.

Shouldn't he be a little upset at least?

His memory still had not returned.

He did not know who he was.

Yes, but he had this time with Lilly, and that mattered more than either of those critical details.

"No, it is not." She presented her profile, gazing out the window. "So, it seems we are back to where we started. Now what?"

TWENTY

Still in Lilly's chilly office

After several unusually loud tick-tocks of the clock

Studying Lilly, Zander canted his head.

Was she relieved or disappointed?

Truth be told, he was both, but what he felt more than anything was adoration for this extraordinary woman.

Surely God would not let him fall in love with this unique, intrepid, and wholly remarkable woman if he were already wedded.

That would be too cruel.

Nevertheless, he had crossed the mark by kissing her in the dining room.

He would not declare himself until he knew for certain that he was a free man.

That would not be honorable or fair to her or his wife—if she existed.

Three short wraps on the door drew their attention.

"Come in," Lilly called, rising and then crossing to her desk to tuck the letter into a drawer.

Eliza slipped inside.

After casting Zander an openly curious glance, she bobbed a little curtsy. "Miss Granger? His lordship, Aldric Davenport, Viscount Merrivale, has called. He asks if you are at home?"

Zander jerked his head up, his stomach coiling into a tight knot.

Why was the viscount here after all this time?

Zander still had not put aside his suspicion that Lilly might be Matilda Davenport's by-blow.

"*Am I at home?*" Lilly repeated, as if thinking out loud. "Aldric Davenport. The son? I was not aware his father had passed."

It was as likely as feathers on fish that this was a social call.

Lilly must have had a similar thought, for three neat lines appeared across her forehead before she schooled her features into her usual benign expression that concealed her inner thoughts.

"Yes, of course, Eliza. Please show his lordship to the drawing room. I shall be there shortly." Her calm, composed response did not fool him.

The viscount's unannounced arrival had thrown her.

Eliza nodded and closed the door behind her.

It did not escape Zander that Lilly had not ordered a tea tray.

Before he could suggest he should accompany Lilly, she faced him. Only the bright, apprehensive gleam in her eyes revealed her disquiet.

"Zander, will you go with me to meet his lordship, please?"

Did she suspect she might need a witness?

Zander would wager his reputation and hers, she very well might.

She inhaled a deep breath before rushing on. "I cannot help but think there is a troublesome purpose behind a visit after all this time."

Smart lass.

"Certainly." He opened the door and waited for her to sweep past him.

As always, he caught a whiff of wildflowers.

With a little encouragement from him, Mrs. B had divulged Lilly did not wear perfume, but she bathed with scented soap—her one indulgence.

He spoke into her ear as they made their way to the drawing room.

"I do not know why he is here, Lilly, but I caution you to speak as little as possible until he reveals his motives. He may simply be curious and want to see what you have done with the place."

That was as likely as the Thames running dry.

Lilly made a noise resembling a grunt.

She was not as unaffected as she pretended.

"His father never once bothered to visit the home." She slid Zander a sideways glance. "Why would his son do so, especially since Miss Davenport has been dead these many years, and according to her, Aldric Davenport, rarely set foot in England?"

Excellent question.

"He did not even return for his mother's funeral." She firmed her pretty mouth. "No, something is afoot."

They had nearly reached the drawing room.

"We shall soon learn his intent." Zander took her elbow. "I am certain he expects you to receive him alone. Let's present a united front, shall we? He will be less inclined to bully."

Her distracted nod and tremulous smile revealed her trepidation.

With Zander by her side, she need not fear

He would champion and defend her.

Zander entered beside Lilly.

Across the room, a tall, well-built man attired in the first stare of fashion stood with his hands behind his back as he stared out the window onto the terrace. He pivoted as Zander and Lilly entered, a half-derogatory, half-self-important smile bending his mouth upward.

Astonishment rendered him speechless for a heartbeat before he strode across the room, a genuine smile of recognition creasing his face.

"Captain Westbrook! I say! This is an unforeseen pleasure." He spared Lilly a cursory glance. "I did not expect to see you here. Last I heard, you were cavorting about in His Majesty's Army."

Zander froze, rooted to the spot.

He closed his eyes as his memory came flooding back, so fast and so overwhelming that dizziness engulfed him. All those fragments he had partially remembered chinked neatly into place to complete the puzzle.

Why he was familiar with women's periodicals, cosmetics, lavender, and herbs—*Grandmama, Libby Westbrook.*

His knowledge of High Society and *le beau monde.*

His abduction and beating by the Earl of Highbury's thugs.

The daring escape he had risked in the dark of night—only he had believed he was heading toward Hexham. Concussed, he must have become turned around during his flight.

Thank God he had.

He opened his eyes.

He never would have met Lilly had he not been confused and fled in the wrong direction.

Making a gruff sound in his throat, he lifted an unsteady hand to his forehead.

"Zander? Are you all right?"

Lilly's worried tone came from far off. She pulled her elbow from his grip and laid her palm on his forearm.

"Zander?"

He blinked to clear his muddled mind and hazy vision—then blinked again as he met her perceptive gaze.

Nay, not Zander.

He was Captain Layton Westbrook, formerly of His Majesty's Army.

And this grinning rake was none other than Aldric Davenport, now the Viscount Merrivale. He had attended Cambridge with Layton's adopted brother, Leonidas.

A frown pulled Merrivale's eyebrows together and turned his mouth downward for a brief moment.

"Zander?" His expression cleared. "Ah, if I recall, Alexander is one of your middle names."

Damned astute of the man because Layton did not have a bloody clue what Merrivale's middle name was and neither did he give a farthing's curse.

"Changed your preferred name, have you? Cannot say that I blame you." Amiable as ever, Merrivale chattered away, seeming not to notice Lilly's shock. "I detest Aldric. Most of my inner circle calls me Rick."

Layton swallowed before giving a shallow nod. "I left the army some time ago. I am currently an instructor at Kelston Hall Children's Home."

That seemed safe enough to divulge.

Lilly's eyes grew impossibly rounder as she must have realized he had regained his memory, but she kept her lips tightly pressed together. Few women would have maintained their composure under these circumstances.

He admired her self-control and poise.

God, his head throbbed like he had been clobbered by an Australian Aboriginal's waddy.

Australian?

Yes, Australian.

Layton had been to Australia for a brief time, delivering confidential dispatches. That explained how he knew about long-neck turtles and gigantic spiders.

Merrivale's eyebrows shot to his hairline in perplexed disbelief.

"You are *employed*...here?"

TWENTY-ONE

In what was now a very uncomfortable drawing room

After the passage of an undeterminable number of awkward seconds

"I am." Layton strove to keep the terseness from his tone, but by God, Merrivale's incredulity bordered on insulting. No, his blatant disbelief radiated disdain.

To a man who had never worked a minute in his life, the shock and disgust were genuine.

"But why, man?" Merrivale glanced around, the faintest hint of contempt flaring his nostrils as he took in the room's simple décor and dismissed the furnishings as commonplace. "You are the adopted son of the wealthy and powerful Duke of Latham, not to mention you possess your own substantial fortune."

True, but that was none of Merrivale's business, and that he knew of Layton's inheritance from his biological father proved more than a little unnerving.

Layton never spoke of his birthright, having despised his

father with every ounce of his being for as long as he could remember. The funds sat in an account at Hoare's Bank, earning a tidy annual income from interest.

He had as much desire to access the funds as he did to be drawn and quartered.

Layton speared Lilly a swift glance.

Her jaw had gone slack before she snapped her mouth closed.

"*Duke*?" she mimed silently, then wandered to stand beside a table displaying several inkwells.

Eyes slightly narrowed, she stared at him reproachfully as she toyed with the lid of a bronze acorn-shaped ink pot.

What the blazes was she thinking?

Surely, she did not blame Layton for what he could not remember until now.

So absorbed in his amazement, Merrivale did not seem to notice. Or more likely, the viscount had dismissed her as an inferior and therefore beneath his regard.

Typical of him.

Aldric Davenport was the epitome of privileged elitist snobbery. Unless blueblood ran in a person's veins, that individual was irrelevant. A nobody.

"Why, by all that is holy, would you *choose* to smell of the shop, Westbrook?"

Merrivale chuckled at his own jest as he wrinkled his nose as if sniffing fresh manure or rotted fish.

"Zounds man, if I had your means, I assuredly would not soil my hands or sully my reputation by engaging in menial service." Merrivale's lip curled upward in derision. "Where is your pride?"

The viscount was such an elitist that it was a wonder the man deemed to wipe his own bum.

As for Layton's pride, much of the overrated emotion had

vanished when his wife had tried to kill him and then ran off with one of his closest friends.

Lilly narrowed her eyes, annoyed sparks shooting from the chocolate irises at Merrivale's string of insults.

What was worse, the self-important coxcomb had no idea how offensive he was.

She curled her fingers around a bronze inkwell as if considering whether to lob it at Merrivale's head.

Layton did not blame her.

"It is all a matter of perspective, is it not?" Layton shrugged and cleared his throat, eager to turn the focus from himself until he spoke with Lilly about his regained memory.

And that he was most certainly *not* married.

Not anymore.

In fact, he was a widower.

A pulse of excitement tunneled through him.

He was free to court Lilly.

At one time, Merrivale's insensitive prattling would have raised Layton's ire, but today, the barbs bounced off before they could prick him.

"I thought you were living abroad, Merrivale." Layton cupped his nape when what he wanted to do was rub his throbbing temples. "I seem to remember Leonidas mentioning he had seen you during his travels. In Morocco, I believe?"

Merrivale's jollity dissipated, and bleakness etched his features.

"My father died a few months ago," he said. "Alas, my life as a wanderer has ended, and I must take up the viscountcies' mantle with all its duties and encumbrances."

While Merrivale had always relished the privileges afforded to a peer's only son, the rapscallion had shirked any responsibilities with a remarkable astuteness.

Until now.

Peculiar, this sudden attentiveness to duty.

Almost as if something beyond self-interest motivated the chap.

That would be a first.

"My sincere condolences, Merrivale."

One of eight siblings, Layton could not fathom the loneliness an only child experienced when his remaining parent died.

Folding her hands, Lilly murmured, "Mine as well, your lordship."

As if he had forgotten she existed, Merrivale glanced over his shoulder toward her. "Yes, and unlike my sire, I take the title seriously."

Since when?

Merrivale had rarely returned to England after his tour of the continent, preferring to whore and gamble his way across Europe and beyond. This sudden commitment to the viscountcy smelled to high heaven.

Something was too smoky by far.

"I have spent months wading through neglected paperwork and meeting with solicitors." Merrivale paused for a half-second before stiffening his spine and thrusting out his noble chin. "Which brings me to why I am here."

At last.

"I have had a man watching Kelston Hall," he announced. "You have quite an industrious operation here, Miss Granger. I am unexpectedly impressed, in truth."

A trace of grudging respect tempered his words.

Layton cocked his head.

And what was Kelston Hall to Merrivale that he would hire someone to observe the estate's operations?

"That was *your* man?" Lilly cut Layton a relieved glance. "I feared he was someone more nefarious."

Layton scowled.

Did she fear the prowler might be one of the ruffians who had abducted him?

"Lilly, you knew someone was lurking about, and you did not tell me?" Layton tempered his astonishment and ire but could not quite keep the accusation from his tone.

"I was not certain he was watching the house, nor did I know his purpose." She shrugged. "I did not want to trouble you."

"I have no idea what you two are blathering on about." The viscount glanced between Layton and Lilly before pinning her with his haughtiest you-are-an-insignificant-insect glare. "But can we get back to the matter at hand?"

Merrivale was not even aware he was a pompous prick.

Regardless, fury simmered inside Layton for the disparaging way the viscount treated Lilly.

"Tread lightly, Merrivale," Layton warned with cold calm. "We might be old acquaintances, but I insist you pay Miss Granger the respect she is due."

"Do not work yourself into a lather, Westbrook." Merrivale gave a dismissive flick of his hand, a sardonic smile curling his upper lip once more. "My business is with Miss Granger. I have no quarrel with you."

Such a condescending assling.

Arms folded, Layton leveled the viscount with a steely glare. "Nor I you."

Yet.

"Please join me for a tankard or two in Prudhoe after I am finished here," Merrivale invited as if they were old chums. "We can catch up on old times."

Her expression pinched, Lilly looked between the men.

Then, as if he were discussing something as banal as the weather, Merrivale turned to her. "I am doing you the courtesy of informing you that I am contesting Aunt Matilda's will. No illegitimate children should have ever been permitted to inherit her estate."

Ah, hell.

"What exactly are you implying, your lordship?" Lilly clasped her hands together, the knuckles white as every ounce of color drained from her face.

"I am not implying anything. I am stating facts," Merrivale scoffed. "You are Aunt Matilda's bastard daughter, and Charles Montrose is my father's by-blow."

Layton had suspected the former, but the latter left him thunderstruck.

Charles and Lilly were cousins.

Now Layton understood the late Miss Davenport's benevolence. She had done everything in her power to protect and provide for her daughter and nephew.

The viscount raked a contemptuous glance over Lilly, but she met his haughty perusal with a direct, unflinching gaze.

Bravo, sweetheart.

"I presume yours and Montrose's surnames are those of your father and his mother," Merrivale said. "Surely, as a peer yourself, you understand why this travesty must not be allowed to continue, Westbrook."

Wiping the floor with Merrivale's face will not help Lilly, Layton scolded himself. *Nor will pummeling him into next year.*

Far better, if wholly less satisfying, for Merrivale to believe Layton's loyalty lay along the same path, though Layton's allegiance was now, and would always remain, to Lilly.

"I understand, Merrivale, that you have given Miss Granger quite a shock."

Layton strode to the door.

He would much rather have gone to Lilly, but mindful that doing so might give Merrivale the wrong impression while providing the viscount fodder for fuel, Layton refrained.

"I think it is time you took your leave, Merrivale, and allow Miss Granger time to digest what you have sprung upon her. I shall accept your invitation and join you. There's not a drop of spirits to be had in the house, and I would welcome a dram."

Perhaps Layton could learn more about the viscount's plans after he had plied the boor with a few drinks.

"As would I." Merrivale gave a curt nod as he presented his back to Lilly.

"What is this world coming to, I ask you, Westbrook?" Merrivale paused at the entrance. As if Lilly was not standing a few feet away, he scoffed, "Neither Aunt Matilda's nor father's illegitimate offspring should ever have inherited a damned farthing."

TWENTY-TWO

Lilly's office

Half five the next morning

Arms wrapped around herself against the early morning chill, Lilly paced across the time-worn Brinston carpet in front of her desk, then, reaching the room's far side, pivoted and retraced her steps. Despite not sleeping more than an hour last night, her mind was sharp as she assessed scenario after scenario for how to deal with Lord Merrivale before discarding it as impractical.

Never had she been so frustrated in her life.

Nor so scared.

So many lives depended upon her, and Charles, of course. But he wasn't responsible for the children's home day-to-day operations. Those duties fell to her, and so did finding a solution to the bumblebroth his lordship had stirred up.

How dare Lord Merrivale show up after all these years and announce that he was contesting his aunt's will?

So smug.

So self-assured.

So blasted certain that Lilly would capitulate without a struggle because a peer had threatened her.

He would soon find she would not surrender without a fight.

Lord, how she had itched to wipe the smirk off his arrogant face, but too much was at stake. At all costs, Lilly must maintain her poise and battle the viscount with intelligence, strategy, and cunning.

She did not doubt that if Miss Davenport's will had not been legal, Lilly and Charles would never have received the inheritance.

The will had been valid.

Accustomed to and familiar with men's shenanigans, Matilda Davenport had made certain her last wishes were carried out.

Too deuced bad if the new Viscount Merrivale objected to his aunt's decision.

Regardless, his lordship meant to take Lilly and Charles to court if they did not hand over Kelston Hall and the remaining funds.

He had said as much yesterday, just before he departed, the greedy bugger.

Away on a call, Charles did not even know what had occurred yet.

Merrivale's demands would destroy the home, the children...And Lilly.

She could not afford a lengthy court battle, and the viscount probably gambled on that. But then, neither could his lordship, or else why would he be so desperate to get his hands on his aunt's estate?

Unless he was simply a greedy bugger who could not stand

the notion of anyone who was born illegitimate, inheriting a fortune.

At the first opportunity, she intended to have a conversation with Zander regarding Lord Merrivale and see what he knew about the viscount.

Not Zander.

His name is Layton.

Captain Layton Westbrook, to be precise.

Adopted son of the Duke of Latham.

Even in Prudhoe, people knew of the prestigious duke.

It had been all she could do to keep from gasping out loud when Merrivale recognized Layton and blurted his connections.

And to think; she had stupidly fallen in love with him.

Thank God, she had never declared herself, for dukes' sons —adopted or not—did not marry illegitimate schoolteachers.

Marry?

There she went again; putting the cart before the horse.

Lack of sleep had muddled her common sense.

Lilly had always prided herself on her levelheadedness and reason, and she did not like in the least feeling discomposed.

A shiver scuttled up her spine despite her heavy shawl.

October had turned quite cold.

She puckered her forehead.

Why hadn't the Westbrooks looked for Layton? A family that powerful had far-reaching influence. Something did not add up, but that was not Lilly's chief concern right now.

Figuring out how to outfox Merrivale was.

Everyone knew the courts favored peers over commoners. Bribing judges was as commonplace as beggars on London's streets.

There must be another way to outwit Lord Merrivale.

But what?

She swiveled again, rubbing her hands up and down her shawl-covered arms. Normally on such a chilly morning, she would have lit a fire, but now she must save every cent she could.

At least Lilly knew why Miss Davenport had paid her and Charles such marked attention.

No wonder Lilly and Charles had such a keen connection.

Likely, she would never know why Miss Davenport had given Lilly and Charles the surnames they had. As with most illegitimate children, their births probably were not recorded anywhere. Despite how Lilly had learned about hers and Charles's kinship, the knowledge was a bright spot in the otherwise sordid tale.

It took a remarkable woman to care for her brother's by-blow, but Matilda Davenport had been an exceptional woman by any standard.

Lilly wished her mother had been brave enough to tell her the truth.

Nevertheless, Lilly could not judge or be angry with her.

In a cruel, unforgiving world where appearances counted for everything, Matilda Davenport had done her best to provide for Lilly and Charles. Besides, Lilly did not know, nor was she likely to ever know, the circumstances that drove Miss Davenport to such extreme measures.

Lilly would always be grateful to the kind, lovely-smelling woman.

Merrivale, the arrogant rotter, had not even cared to stay and meet Charles—his only brother, and he had treated Lilly, his only cousin as if she were vermin. A filthy rug to wipe his muddy boots upon.

Not that he'd had much choice in the matter.

A reluctant smile bent her mouth upward.

Likely guessing Lilly was on the cusp of boxing Lord Merrivale's ears, Layton had agreed to join the viscount for a tankard or two in the village and bustled his lordship out the door before she could hurl an inkpot at the viscount's head.

Layton still had not returned when Lilly finally went to bed at half midnight.

Sighing, she rolled her stiff shoulders, attempting to dispel what felt like a heavy oxen yoke weighing her down. Her burden was hefty because she cared so much for the children and staff, and what would happen to them if—God forbid—Merrivale succeeded in his vile mission?

Lilly might as well head to the kitchen and make a pot of tea. She would need several cups to stay alert after her sleepless night. And she needed her wits about her when she encountered Layton today.

What would she say to him?

Everything had changed between them.

She pressed her chilly hands to her suddenly flaming cheeks.

Lord, she had kissed him like an immoral wanton.

Dunderhead.

Dolt.

Simpleton.

Castigating herself as she made her way to the kitchen, Lilly faltered just outside the doorway. A light glowed from within.

Who was up before her?

Adjusting her shawl, she entered.

The distinct, pleasant aroma of rising bread teased her nostrils.

Mrs. B sat at the kitchen table, an untouched cup of tea, steam spiraling upward in front of her. Narrow shoulders slumped, she sniffled and dabbed at her lowered face.

Alarm washed through Lilly as she rushed across the cold stones.

"Mrs. B? Whatever is wrong.

"Why are you here so early?

"Didn't you spend the night in Prudhoe with your ailing sister-in-law?"

Mrs. B lifted her startled, tear-dampened face.

"Mercy, Lilly. You gave me a fright." She pressed a hand to her thin chest. "Why are you up so early?"

"I could not sleep." Lilly slid into the chair next to Mrs. B and took the housekeeper's gnarled hand in hers. "Did your sister-in-law pass away?"

"Lord, no. Trudy has a severe case of gout." Shaking her silvery head, Mrs. B gave her a watery smile. "She is too stubborn to change her diet and suffers for her obstinance, but she is a long way from turning up her toes. She is not called moody Trudy for no reason."

"Why are you crying, then?" Lilly scanned her dear face for signs of sickness or fever. "Are you ill?"

"I am quite well, just a silly old woman." Mrs. B swiped at her wrinkled face. Despair etched upon her wizened features, she stared out the window into the predawn darkness.

Lilly wrapped an arm around the tiny woman's shoulders. "Please tell me what is wrong."

"These tears are not for me, deary," Mrs. B murmured. "They are for you."

"*Me*?" Lilly squeezed her shoulder. "Ah, I presume you have heard about Miss Davenport being my mother, and that Charles is my cousin, the illegitimate son of the former Viscount Merrivale."

Lilly doubted she would ever become accustomed to thinking of the woman as her mother.

In the process of blowing her nose, Mrs. B stopped, her eyes going round as silver platters. "She was? He is? Well, tickle me pink and call me a dandy."

"You did not know?" Mrs. B was always aware of everything that went on in the house. Lilly furrowed her forehead. "Then why are you weeping?"

Mrs. B finished blowing her nose—noisily and thoroughly.

Tears well in her eyes again. "Because, my dear, Zander has left us, and I am not blind. I know how fond you had grown of him."

What?

Lilly's shock must have registered on her face. Had she been so dashed obvious, despite trying her best to hide her feelings?

She swallowed the lump in her throat. "How... How do you know he left?"

"I heard the news from Trudy's daughter-in-law when she arrived to relieve me this morning." Mrs. B's shoulders slumped.

He's gone.

Layton is gone.

"My nephew, Tupp told her." Sympathy creased Mrs. B's weathered face. "There was a kerfuffle at *The Crown and Stone* last night, you see, while Tupp was enjoying a pint."

Surely, Mrs. B heard every jagged crack cleaving Lilly's heart.

Lilly shook her head, confusion and something much more powerful befuddling her thoughts. "What do you mean he has left us? He would not do that. Just leave."

Without even saying goodbye?

Would he?

He would if he is married, her cool, logical self, chastised her.

"That is exactly what I said too." Mrs. B gazed at her intently. "Tupp said, Zander arrived at the pub with a posh gent..."

"Viscount Merrivale," Lilly interjected, her voice raspy

with suppressed emotion. "He was here yesterday to tell me he is contesting Miss Davenport's will."

Mrs. B stiffened in outrage. "He cannot do that, can he?"

"That remains to be seen." Lilly sucked in a steadying breath. "So that I would not pop the bounder's arrogant cork, Layton—that is Zander's real name, Captain Layton Westbrook—took the viscount to Prudhoe for a tankard."

The viscount's arrival had sparked Zander—that was, Layton's memory.

Lilly had seen it clearly when he had opened his eyes and met her gaze.

Mrs. B's eyes glowed brightly with unshed tears. "According to Tupp, a couple of ruffians looking for trouble wandered into the pub. There was an altercation between them, the viscount, and our captain. They knocked the toff out, straightaway."

She grinned, exposing her missing teeth.

"Tupp says, Zander, I mean Captain Westbrook," she rushed to correct, "gave the two blokes a proper drubbing, before carrying his lordship to the viscount's smart carriage, depositing him inside, and telling the driver to drive hell-bent for leather to London."

He left me.

Legs shaking so badly Lilly was not positive she could stand, she pushed herself to her feet. She gripped the table's edge with white-knuckled fingers, willing her knees not to buckle under the weight of her grief and disbelief. "I ...I need some air."

"Lilly...? Dear?" Worry rendered Mrs. B's voice wobbly. "Please tell me. What can I do?"

Lilly waved her hand, not trusting herself to speak.

She forced one foot in front of the other until she reached the kitchen garden entrance. She fumbled with the handle before finally wrenching the door open.

Frigid pre-dawn air stalled Lilly's breath, but she welcomed the briskness stinging her cheeks and eyes.

"Lilly?" Mrs. B called again.

Tears leaked from the corners of Lilly's eyes, and she bit her lower lip hard to suppress the primal cry of agony clawing at her throat.

She picked up her skirts and ran.

And ran.

And ran.

Lilly pelted past the stables and the orchard.

One cow mooed a sleepy welcome, but Lilly didn't slow her pace.

She dashed past the pond and the oak grove.

With each step, she berated and castigated herself.

Lackwit.

Gudgeon.

Clodpole.

Addlepate.

She sprinted until her lungs burned and her breath came in great wheezing gasps, and then, unable to take another step, she folded to her knees on the dew-covered ground.

It was only then that she realized her traitorous feet had carried her to the very place where Layton had been discovered those many weeks ago.

Oh, God. Oh, God.

A wail more suited to a mortally wounded animal tore itself from her throat, and she collapsed into a heap, curling her fingernails into the damp soil.

He is gone.

He is gone.

I shall never see my love again.

Lilly's heart splintered, and she almost swooned from the agony spearing her.

She wanted to faint, to escape the pain eviscerating her.

Curling into a fetal position, she sobbed uncontrollably, despising herself for her weakness, but unable to wrestle her grief under control. She did not know how much time passed as she lay there, wounded and mind numb, but eventually, the reservoir of her tears ran dry.

She should return to the house to restore her appearance before the students and staff roused for the day. Still, she could not muster a jot of motivation to move.

The light had gone out of her—no, the light of her life had left her—and she didn't know how she would go on. And despite her brokenness, she could not help but fear for Layton's safety.

Did the men who had abducted him still pose a risk?

A short while later, Charles found her and wordlessly gathered her shivering form into his arms.

"He is gone, Charles," she murmured through cold-stiffened lips. "He did not even bid me farewell."

"I know, sweetheart." Pressing his cheek into her hair, he rocked her as if she were a toddler in need of soothing. "Mrs. B told me what happened. I am sorrier than I can say, Lil."

So am I.

I loved him—love him.

And he left me without a second thought.

"After speaking with Mrs. B, and learning Zander is Captain Layton Westbrook, I suddenly remembered what had been niggling my conscience all this while." Releasing a pent-up breath, he sighed. "A few weeks ago, on one of my calls to another village, someone mentioned that several aristocrats had been nosing around, asking questions about their missing brother."

So, his family had searched for him, after all.

Charles gave Lilly an apologetic smile. "I regret that I did not recall that before now."

Because Layton's identity would have been discovered sooner, possibly saving her a broken heart.

"It is of no consequence, Charles."

Apparently, Captain Layton Westbrook was cut from the same cloth as Viscount Merrivale. Layton's abrupt change in behavior once he knew who he was should not have surprised her, and that it did, made her a colossal dunderhead.

What exactly had he remembered?

That he *was* married?

A rusty, serrated knife twisting in Lilly's heart would not have caused more pain than that thought.

"Let's get you home, and warmed, shall we?" Charles kissed the crown of her head.

Yes.

Lilly had responsibilities.

She must focus on her duties and obligations.

Take her heels-tossed-over-bum-life one minute at a time.

Wallowing in self-pity served no purpose. It would not bring Layton back, and it would not help her concoct a plan to thwart Lord Merrivale.

A rooster crowed, announcing dawn's arrival with a soft silvery light filtering through the mist-laden fields.

Sucking in a ragged breath, she nodded.

If Layton could leave her so easily, after that sizzling kiss, well then, she would put him from her mind too.

Lilly would focus all her energy on saving the children's home.

Charles helped her stand.

"Lilly, I am sure he had good reason—"

Like a wife?

Lilly held up her hand, palm outward, cutting him off.

Anguish slashed her heart.

She must put Layton out of her mind. Erect an impenetrable barricade if she were to survive this devastation brought on by her naivete.

"We shall return to our lives before he came, Charles, and never speak of him again."

Charles could not hide his amazement, and the compassion that filled his eyes nearly undid her.

He gave a curt nod. "As you wish."

Lilly accepted the elbow he extended.

Dear Charles. At least she still had him.

I shall never trust my heart again.

TWENTY-THREE

De la Chance's breakfast room
London, England

27 October 1828—before dawn

I miss you, Lilly, my love. My heart.

Slouched in a chair, wearing only black pantaloons and an untucked lawn shirt with the sleeves rolled to his elbows, Layton propped his stocking feet on the gold brocade upholstered chair beside him. He scraped a hand through his mussy hair, then took a large swig of strong, black coffee.

Staring out the breakfast room window into London's dark early morn, he angled his head, listening as the town came fully awake.

The city's constant noise filtered inside his brother Fletcher's prestigious club's private quarters; an unwelcome and stark contrast to Kelston Hall's serenity. Until now, Layton had not realized how much he disliked London's bustle and hubbub or how much he craved the countryside's peace and solitude.

He had been a soldier for decades and duty took him wherever His Majesty dictated. His preference for locations was irrelevant when carrying out his orders. But now that he was a civilian once more, he could choose where he wanted to be.

And he would pick bucolic locations every time.

Oddly, the city's never-ending commotion reminded him of Virginia, his dead wife. She was never happy or content, but always flighty, agitated, and disgruntled. Considered a diamond of the first water when Layton had married her, her outward beauty and blueblood could not compensate for her greedy, adulterous heart.

Strange how, at six and twenty, he had been positive his love would be enough to ensure their happy union, despite his parents' considerable reservations about the match.

Time had proven him wrong.

So bloody wrong.

Not only had Virginia proven a promiscuous tart, but she conspired to kill him, so she could claim his inheritance from his biological father. Though blinded in one eye, Layton had survived the explosion, and Virginia and her current lover, another army officer, had fled.

Layton had not shed a single tear when they died in a coach accident during their flight. Instead, he had closed his heart to love, vowing to never trust another woman.

Crossing his ankles, he grazed his fingertips across the stubble covering his lower face.

If it had not been for his abduction and amnesia, he would not have allowed himself to fall in love with Lilly.

In that respect, Highbury's hired thugs had done him a colossal favor.

Just thinking of her brought him joy and happiness that he had never anticipated feeling again.

How was she?

Worried?

Angry?

Disillusioned?

Afraid?

Layton's heart twinged with renewed remorse for the hasty manner in which he had departed Prudhoe ten days ago, but he had been given no choice.

He closed his eyes, picturing her standing in Kelston Hall's drawing room, uncertain and vulnerable, yet her brown eyes filled with trust as he had escorted Viscount Merrivale from the room.

A wry half-smile tugged his mouth upward on one side as he opened his eye. Truth be told, he was quite proud of himself for not pummeling the viscount for disparaging Lilly.

Regardless, Layton would bet his remaining good eye that trust no longer glimmered in her doe-eyed gaze. In all likelihood, Lilly believed he had abandoned her, when that was the farthest thing from the truth.

His abrupt leave-taking had been to protect her and the children.

Ten days ago, he did not know Highbury and his thugs had already been detained, thanks to his brothers' diligence. That the villains posed no further risk to him, Lilly, or anyone else at Kelston Hall brought him a tremendous sense of relief.

However, until Merrivale had been dealt with once and for all, he thought it wisest to remain near the viscount.

Layton hadn't written her yet to explain his actions, mainly because he preferred to inform Lilly in person, when he could also tell her he was not married. And, as important, how much he adored her.

Nevertheless, that had not stopped him from hiring four men, highly recommended by his step-cousin, Torrian Westbrook, a successful detective, to guard Kelston Hall discreetly during Layton's absence.

He strongly suspected his highhanded actions would miff Lilly, but what she did not know could not upset her. And when they next met—and they would, by thunder, if it was the last thing he ever did—he would explain everything to her and beg her to forgive him.

And ask her to marry him.

He who had sworn off marriage.

The irony did not escape him.

Although, knowing his intrepid, independent Lilly as he did, she would initially refuse his proposal, citing the need to care for the children. Nevertheless, he had a masterful plan to counter her argument.

One, he hoped, she could not say *no* to.

Time would not pass swiftly enough until he saw her precious face again. He even missed the children, Charles, and Mrs. B.

They had become a second family to him.

Soon.

Soon, he could return.

Once Merrivale relinquished any claim to Matilda Davenport's estate. Layton hoped that would occur during his meeting with the viscount tomorrow afternoon.

Heaving a heavy sigh, he set the nearly empty cup aside.

"More coffee, Captain Westbrook?" *De le Chance's* footman asked, looking and sounding far too chipper at this ungodly hour.

What was the cheerful fellow's name?

Humphrey?

Yes, that was it.

"No, thank you, Humphrey." Layton shook his head. The four cups he had already drunk sloshed about in his belly. "I would appreciate something to break my fast, though."

"Of course." Humphrey gave a nod as he collected the

coffee cup. He slid Layton a side-eyed glance. "Do you have any requests?"

"No." Shaking his head, Layton swallowed a yawn. "Something simple. Whatever the cook can toss together."

"Very good, Captain." Humphrey took his leave on silent feet.

All of Fletcher's employees moved about the social club with deft stealthiness, appearing and disappearing almost like specters.

Yawning, Layton closed his eyes.

He was bloody exhausted.

And yet he had endured another sleepless night, rising at just after four to walk off his restlessness among London's dank and cold lanes.

It had not worked.

As always, thoughts of Lilly inundated him.

Sweet Lilly, with her ready smile and keen wit. Her kindness and compassion. Her resilience and fortitude.

God above, how Layton missed her.

Missed the sound of her dulcet voice, her joyful laughter, her clean, refreshing scent. Every minute away from her caused the ache within him to grow.

Once more, he let his mind wander back to that afternoon when he had regained his memory.

At first, he had thought nothing of the drunken troublemakers at the *Crown and Stone.* Inebriated men said and did imbecilic things, and he had witnessed hundreds of sots before, making absolute fools of themselves while pished to the proverbial gills.

But it had soon appeared that the rough pair had not randomly selected the *Crown and Stone* to drown their sorrows. While downing tankard after tankard, through bloodshot eyes, they observed him and Merrivale far too closely for their presence to be happenstance.

Initially, because Layton did not yet know of the Earl of Highbury's arrest, that realization had disturbed him. However, the sods showed nothing more than cursory interest in him, and he had hoped that meant Highbury had given up the chase.

However, as the evening progressed, it became apparent that the thugs were targeting Merrivale, which meant they either had decided he was a rich ponce to rob, or they were henchmen sent to teach him a lesson.

If it had not been for Layton, the scoundrels would likely have succeeded in their mission.

After regaining consciousness on the way to London, and though immensely grateful for Layton's help, Merrivale remained mulishly silent about the matter and would neither deny nor confirm the louts' intent.

No amount of prodding or cajoling had loosened his lordship's lips. The viscount had clamped his mouth shut tighter than a virgin nun's legs.

Regardless, one thing was inarguable.

Merrivale was utterly terrified.

Which probably meant he was involved in something way over his aristocratic head, or he was in trouble up to his starched neckcloth. That also explained his desperation to get his hands on Matilda Davenport's legacy. He had wrongly assumed he could bully Lilly into acquiescence, then probably bribe a magistrate to rule in his favor.

He had not calculated on Layton's presence or interference.

With Fletcher's and Torrian's help, Layton meant to find out exactly what Merrivale was mixed up in, hence his delay in leaving London. He had not even seen his parents yet, though he had sent word to the duke and duchess that he was all right and would come to visit as soon as possible.

Immeasurable relief filled Layton when he learned Cassius

and Beatrice were safe. Their betrothal came as no surprise. They might not have known it themselves, but Layton had concluded while helping them escape to London that the two were head-over-heels in love.

According to Fletcher, the Westbrook family had spent the last several weeks searching for Layton, but someone had thought they spied him near Hexham, and that was where they had focused their search.

"Unable to sleep again, Layton?" Fletcher asked, the merest hint of brotherly concern tempering the question.

Of Layton's six brothers, Fletcher was his only blood kin.

As if Layton had returned from the dead, he had welcomed him exuberantly. In a manner of speaking, Layton had, for he surely would have died had it not been for Lilly and Charles.

Fletcher confessed that after weeks had passed and they had not found Layton, the entire Westbrook family had feared the worst. However, that had not stopped them from hunting down the Earl of Highbury and bringing him and his hirelings to justice.

Layton had been wise to avoid Sheriff Wrottesley.

Though not an accomplice in Layton's abduction, the sheriff was one of Highbury's paid lackeys. Without a qualm or hesitation, he would have reported Layton's location to the earl.

Layton glanced over his shoulder as his brother entered the breakfast room. Stifling a yawn, he shrugged.

"Sleep has not been my friend for many years, Fletch."

Except while Layton stayed at Kelston Hall.

The eagle owls' nocturnal hooting and Hodgson Burn's distant burbling acted as nature's lullaby, easing him into a deep slumber each night. Roosters crowing, cows lowing, sheep baaing, and the ever-present call of the doves roused him from slumber every morning.

Fletcher slipped onto the chair opposite Layton, then nodded his appreciation when Humphrey approached with a cup of steaming, black coffee. "Thank you, Humphrey."

"I have already requested breakfast for Captain Westbrook, sir." The footman adjusted his gold-striped waistcoat. "Should I do the same for you?"

Lifting his cup, Fletcher nodded. "I shall have whatever Cook prepared for my brother. I hope there are croissants. Have a tray sent up for my wife, too, please."

"Very good, sir." Humphrey slipped away once more.

Layton was the last of his siblings to find true love. Soon, there would be another Westbrook bride. *If* he could convince Lilly to marry him.

Inhaling the steam rising from his hot coffee, Fletcher sighed.

"I can never thank you enough for introducing me to Yemen's Mocha coffee, Layton."

Mocha coffee was one of many exotic products Layton had brought back from his military travels.

"For a man who has been all over the world," Fletcher teased, "I still cannot believe you became so turned around that you mistook Prudhoe for Hexham."

Layton raised an eyebrow. "Did I fail to mention I had a concussion and was barely conscious?"

"Nay." Remorse creased Fletcher's face. "I was but jesting."

"I know." Layton did not mind his brother's joking. While he regretted the angst his family had endured when they could not find him, he would never regret getting turned around.

By getting lost, he found himself again.

"What are your plans for today?" Fletcher asked.

"I am paying a call at Hoare's Bank this morning." Layton observed his brother's reaction.

Eyebrows shooting high, Fletcher paused in raising his cup to his mouth. "Oh?"

His casualness did not fool Layton.

He was curious—immensely so—but he did not want to pry.

"I have decided to put our father's money to good use," Layton said.

Fletcher chuckled in approval. "Bravo. It is about time."

After leaving the field of medicine, having found a career as a physician too emotionally taxing, Fletcher used his share of their inheritance to establish several successful businesses.

He rested his forearms on the table and leaned forward. "Would I be too presumptuous in asking what you intend to do with the funds?"

"Not at all, though you may not approve." Layton returned his brother's grin.

Fletcher's keen attention never wavered. "Try me."

"I am creating a trust fund for Kelston Hall Children's Home to be managed by its director, Lilibet Granger."

"A worthy cause, to be sure, and I am not entirely surprised." Fletcher leaned back, his too-astute attention boring into Layton. "I seem to remember at one time you considered adopting. Is that still the case?"

"I grew quite fond of the children at the home while I was there." Layton could do more than adopt a child or two or four. He could use his inheritance to help many children. "Miss Granger has expressed an interest in expanding her operation. Now she can."

And hopefully, Layton would be by her side through it all.

"I am not stupid, Layton." His hand encircling his coffee cup, Fletcher pointed his forefinger toward Layton. "I know Miss Granger is much more to you than just the home's director."

"She saved my life." Layton dropped his focus to the table

for a moment, then raised his gaze. "I love her, and I want to marry her, if she will have me."

"I could not be happier, brother." Fletcher beamed. "Of course, she will have you."

Layton wished he was as confident.

Fletcher leaned forward again, elbows on the table. "Now let me tell you what I learned about Viscount Merrivale last night."

TWENTY-FOUR

Kelston Hall's courtyard

5 November 1828—evening
Guy Fawkes night

A sharp, loud bang rent the chilly night, followed by crackling and sparks shooting five feet into the air. Exuberant clapping drowned out the children's excited chorus of *oohs* and *aahs*, and a few startled shrieks from the adults present as well.

Smiling at their enthusiasm, Lilly adjusted the hand-knitted scarf around her neck.

This had been a wonderful decision, despite the added expense, which she had paid for with her savings. Besides, the children's home was not destitute yet.

Layton's sudden departure had affected the boys and girls far more than she had expected, and Lilly hoped the extra celebrations would lift them from their doldrums.

They did little to raise her spirits, but she refused to let anyone see her desolation.

Mourning his absence was pointless, anyway.

Returning Nellie's excited wave from the other side of the roaring bonfire, Lilly roved her attention over those assembled here tonight.

These people were her family, and she loved them.

Yes, she was sad and missed Layton beyond words, but her heart would heal in time.

At least, she prayed it would.

Tonight, she was determined to enjoy herself.

A favorite holiday of the children and staff, every year, Kelston Hall Children's School celebrated Guy Fawkes Night with a bonfire, roasted chestnuts, hot spiced cider, and toffee apples.

However, this year, Lilly had splurged and asked Charles to purchase several squibs. She had drawn the line at permitting the children to hold handheld firebrands as being too dangerous, even if the village children were wont to run amuck while holding them and screeching at the top of their lungs.

As another special treat, Mrs. B had spent most of yesterday making treacle toffee. Lilly and the teachers had supervised the children in creating Guy Fawkes effigies from straw and old rags. In truth, it was a rather barbaric practice to toss the effigies into the fire, but then mankind was rather barbaric.

Wasn't that why men believed themselves superior to women for no reason other than they possessed different genitalia? Or why men made almost all the important decisions, and women were supposed to submit and agree without a word of objection?

Why aristocrats like Viscount Merrivale thought he could snap his manicured fingers, and she, born on the wrong side of the blanket, would agree to his demands?

The pompous boor.

Life was wholly unfair.

Every day now, she dreaded going through the post, expecting a letter from his lordship or a solicitor on his behalf.

So far, no correspondence had arrived from either, and that was most peculiar.

As agitated as Lord Merrivale had been that afternoon, Lilly was at a loss to understand his continued silence.

And Layton's.

Shouldn't the pain from his continued silence diminish with each passing day?

It had not.

How could Lilly heal if she could not stop thinking about him?

Dreaming about him?

Her conclusion that he was married must be accurate, and that explained why he had not written to her.

Layton was a man of integrity.

She had known that about him even before she knew his true identity.

Corresponding with an unmarried woman could be considered inappropriate, and he would never dishonor his wife—even if he had kissed Lilly.

He had done so, not knowing who he was or if he was married.

Lilly should regret that wonderful kiss, but she could not.

No, she *would* not.

It was a gift she would always treasure.

Inhaling a bracing breath, she glanced upward, grateful the pleasant weather had held. Stars sparkled overhead in the inky night sky.

This was a good life.

Before Layton had arrived, she had been content.

More than content.

She had been happy.

Lilly would be so again.

She was determined to make it so.

Hadn't the philosopher Seneca said, "A wise man is content with his lot, whatever it may be, without wishing for what he has not?"

Well, somehow, Lilly would create her happiness, though that would be easier done without the albatross of Lord Merrivale's threat looming overhead.

"Again, Dr. Montrose. Again," the children chanted.

Hopping up and down, the boys and girls danced about giddily as Charles, several feet away for safety, lit another squib.

Miss McKenzie, Miss Wobblecroft, and Mrs. Jones sipped hot spiced cider and wandered among the children, ensuring they had fun but did not get into mischief.

After having brought out the food and arranged it on a large table, the other staff warmed themselves before the enormous fire.

More exuberant cries filled the air as the squib exploded.

"Look!" Mrs. Jones pointed toward Prudhoe.

As one, the children and staff faced the village, and a collective gasp went up.

Orange, yellow, and white fireworks exploded in the sky over what must be the village green.

The majestic display even enthralled Lilly.

"Hello, Lilly."

No, *he* could not be here.

She froze, certain her ears played tricks on her.

After all, a cacophony of noises filled the night.

She missed Layton so much that she had conjured his voice.

That was all.

"Lilly?"

A moment later, his firm hand cupped her shoulder and rotated her toward him.

Oh, God.

She had not imagined that familiar baritone.

Heart hammering against her ribs, she dragged her focus upward from his slightly dusty Wellington boots, past the hem of his slate-blue woolen caped greatcoat, and upward from each brass button to the coat's stiff, turned-up collar, to rest on his strong, square chin, covered with a dark shadowing of whiskers.

"Look at me, Lilly. Please."

Such tenderness filled his husky voice; tears filled her eyes.

Taking in every contour of his beloved face, she continued the upward journey until she met his eye.

Layton was here.

Why?

She darted a wary glance past him.

No stunning beauty stood there, dressed in the first stare of fashion, and gazing at him with utter adoration.

Where was his wife?

"Hello," he murmured.

One word.

One paltry word and Lilly's world suddenly grew bright with hope once more.

His smile would have melted an iceberg, and Lilly assuredly was not a frozen ice-mountain. She was a flesh and blood woman, and if he kept looking at her like that, she would dissolve into a puddle at his feet or burst into flames.

Neither made an ounce of sense, but her reason seemed to have deserted her—flown away on the evening breeze to join the stars overhead. Her blasted knees refused to stop shaking, and her heart beat frantically, like a caged bird trying to escape its gilded prison.

"Hello," she echoed stupidly, for her tongue had not caught up to her racing mind.

He touched her cheek with his forefinger, and even

through the cold leather of his black glove, the spot burned hot. "I missed you."

She had missed him too.

So very much.

"Mr. Brook! Mr. Brook!"

"He came. Mr. Brook is here."

The children had spotted Layton and raced toward him.

Lilly must tell them Layton's real name and that they should address him as Captain Westbrook. But that could wait.

Miss Wobblecroft raised her voice. "Be careful, children."

"Slow down," called Miss McKenzie from Charles's side.

Her cheeks appeared rather more flushed than could be attributed to the roaring bonfire.

"Don't trip and fall into the fire," warned Mrs. Jones as she hurried forward, still clutching her spiced cider.

Layton gave Lilly a sideways grin and winked. "I suppose privacy is too much to ask for."

Privacy?

Was he serious?

With this many children?

"No, privacy is a rare commodity around here." She shook her head.

"There are worse things. I shall figure out a way to have you to myself," he said.

Did that mean he intended to stay?

Was it truly possible?

For how long?

Caught up in the moment, Lilly laughed. "Not likely unless we lock ourselves away somewhere."

"That could be arranged." The glint in his gray eye held a sensual promise.

Yes, she was definitely going to go up in flames.

Before she could respond, the children were upon them.

He looked over their heads and, grinning, mouthed, "Later."

Be careful.

Do not read something into this that is not there.

Lilly pressed her lips together against her reflexive smile.

She had learned her lesson.

Until she knew why Layton had returned, she had no intention of lowering her defenses.

TWENTY-FIVE

Kelson Hall's terrace

Close to midnight that same night

Layton quietly slipped onto the terrace and glanced about. A mantle of crystalline frost covered the stones and grounds, turning the estate into a sparkling fairyland.

He quirked his mouth into a self-deprecating smile.

Since when did he, the toughened war veteran and hard-hearted cynic, wax poetic?

Since he had found true love.

"I am over here."

Lilly's sweet voice drifted to him from farther down the verandah.

She stepped from the shadows, and he quickened his pace to meet her.

Stopping before her, he swept his gaze over her upturned face.

Such a beloved face.

"Hello, again."

A reluctant smile arched her mouth. "Hello."

At some point during the chaos of the rest of the Guy Fawkes Night celebrations, he had whispered in her ear for her to meet him on the terrace once everyone was abed.

In truth, Layton had not been positive she would sneak outside for a clandestine rendezvous, for she had become distinctly cooler toward him after their initial meeting.

Not that he could fault her trepidation.

After all, she had a reputation to preserve.

Had she not shown up, he would have understood and found another time to speak with her alone.

He was impatient to declare himself, to assure her of his love and devotion.

Their breath formed miniature vapor clouds in the frigid air, yet with the inferno blazing inside him, Layton did not feel the chill.

Love did that to a chap.

Turned warriors into sentimental wretches.

Aye, and it was worth the suffering for the love of a woman like Lilly.

He cradled her cold cheek in the palm of his hand.

She should not remain out here in this frigid night air for long, but at least she need not worry he intended to seduce her.

"I missed you, Lilly."

Those four paltry words did not begin to express his powerful emotions.

Bending his neck, Layton touched her forehead with his and inhaled her wildflower scent.

This overwhelming tenderness he felt for her might well emasculate him, but he did not care. "I am sorry I did not say goodbye. Circumstances prevented me from doing so, but I know I hurt you."

Surrounded by the silent night, she stepped backward, searching his face in the dim light.

"Why did you come back, Layton?"

A steely thread laced her soft question.

That was Lilly.

All pragmatic and sensible.

And she'd had time to erect a defense to protect herself against further pain.

A bold declaration about a future together might not be the best approach at this moment.

Instead, he sought to reassure her.

He cupped her shoulders, peering into her wary eyes.

"First, you must know. I am not married, Lilly. I was, several years ago, but she died."

She did not need to know those unpleasant details right now. Of course, Layton would tell her.

There would be no secrets between them. Ever.

The darkness made it impossible to see for certain, but he thought relief may have swept across her beloved face.

Still, she remained silent, staring at him with those enormous eyes.

Layton understood her silent question.

That he was not married did not explain his return to Kelston Hall, nor why he had asked her to meet him tonight. Was it possible that his strong, spirited, independent Lilly was afraid to ask what was in her heart?

"While in London, I learned my abductors had been caught and imprisoned." He had already sent word for the men he hired to watch Kelston Hall to take their leave. "There is no need to worry about them any longer."

No need to talk to Wrottesley either.

Layton had learned of the lascivious rapscallion's reputation and did not want the sheriff anywhere near Lilly.

"That is a relief. I had worried..." As if Lilly revealed too much, she cast a forlorn glance toward the silvery meadows, then shrugged as she shook her head. "'Tis of no matter."

It mattered.

She regarded him warily again. "You could have written and told me those things, Layton."

"I could have, yes, but I wanted to tell you in person." He smiled at her tenderly, so reserved and guarded. "I have created a trust for Kelston Hall and made you the trustee."

Layton would start there and see where the conversation led.

That surprised her, and she tilted her head like an inquisitive little wren. "Why would you do that, and where did the funds come from?"

Her reticence was not unexpected, and he had prepared a defense.

"I used the inheritance from my father. He was not an honorable man, and from a very early age, I determined I would only ever use the money for a benevolent cause and never for my benefit."

The years of anger Layton had harbored toward his father dissolved when he signed the trust documents. Finally, free of the encumbrance of resentment, he looked forward to the good Lilly would do with the money.

The wind had increased, teasing the loose strands of hair around her face and whipping the hems of his greatcoat and her cloak.

The chill in the air quickly stripped the night of its magical qualities.

"That is magnanimous of you, but I wish you had spoken to me first." She brushed a flaxen hair from her face. "Especially with the ongoing issue with Lord Merrivale."

Layton shifted so that his body partially blocked the wind from reaching her.

"Merrivale is no longer a problem. In fact, he left the

country on a ship bound for Morocco, and I do not know if or when he will return."

"Why do I think you had something to do with that?" Shivering, she crossed her arms.

Layton could conceal nothing from her, nor did he have any desire to.

"You are right. My brother, Fletcher, owns a gaming club in London. He discovered that Merrivale owed a substantial debt in Morocco. The viscount borrowed funds from nefarious sources in England to temporarily pacify the debt holder, but the moneylenders became impatient when he did not promptly repay the loans. Merrivale had no idea the viscountcy was in such dire straits, and out of desperation, he thought he would contest his aunt's will."

Lilly made a sound in her throat—perhaps, an inaudible protest against the penetrating cold or her disdainful opinion of the viscount.

"You should know, Lilly, Matilda Davenport's will is undisputable," Layton assured her. While in London, he hired multiple solicitors to research the issue. "It would have held up in court."

"I thought as much, but that does not mean the battle would not have been intense and expensive." She lowered her chin, huddling into her cloak. "The cost could have bankrupted Charles and me. How would I have taken care of the children then?"

"Thankfully, that is no longer a worry." Layton pulled the collar of his coat higher.

The wind and frigid air seemed intent on creeping into every opening.

Lilly pressed her pretty lips together in disapproval. "I do not have much sympathy for a man who incurs gambling debts, especially when he threatens the wellbeing of the children I care for. Still, what has that to do with you or the viscount's departure from England?"

"It was not a gambling debt." Layton raised her chin with his forefinger. "For years, Merrivale has been trying to buy the freedom of a European woman captured by corsairs and enslaved in Morocco who he had fallen in love with."

Gasping, she jerked her head up. "That's utterly barbaric. That poor woman."

Layton's estimation of the viscount had risen considerably upon learning that distasteful detail. It seemed Aldric Davenport was not the snob Layton believed him to be.

"I agree wholeheartedly." Layton gave a terse nod.

He had firsthand knowledge of just how barbaric and common such practices were.

"Her Arabic owner finally agreed to let Merrivale buy her when the viscount learned his father had died. Merrivale made a down payment, with the agreement he would pay the debt in full when he returned from England after settling his father's estate."

"And when he started sorting through the previous viscount's affairs, he realized there was no money." Sympathy tempered Lilly's words now. "What an awful situation. I can imagine he was completely overwrought. I presume you gave him the funds he needed to free her fully?"

"I did." He gave a terse nod. "Only after I made him sign a contract guaranteeing he would never attempt to dispute Matilda Davenport's will again."

An appreciative smile bent her mouth upward.

"It seems I have much to thank you for, Layton. Not only do I no longer have to fret about Lord Merrivale, but you have generously provided additional security for the children's home." She touched his arm. "I am grateful."

He edged nearer.

"It is not your gratitude I want, Lilly."

Emotion rendered his voice gravelly.

"I want you."

Her stunned silence gave him hope, or mayhap, sheer desperation made him plow onward, seizing the opportunity.

"I love you. I want to marry you and have little ones together." He cupped her satiny cheeks between his palms. "I want to help you with the children's home because until I met you, I was only half alive."

"I am freezing, Layton."

Now it was his turn to be stunned.

That assuredly was not the response he had anticipated or hoped for at all.

Although he had expected her to argue about one or two points, at least—she would not be Lilly if she didn't—he had prayed she would throw herself into his arms and declare her love for him too.

She did love him, didn't she?

She must.

Layton's joy plummeted to his frozen toes and perished.

"Let's go inside, shall we?" She slipped her icy hand into his.

What is this?

A kernel of hope flickered to life.

As Lilly led him toward the drawing room's terrace doors, she slid him a siren's smile. "I am certain we can find a clever way to warm ourselves."

The kernel sparked and became a low-burning flame.

Did his prim and proper headmistress imply what Layton thought she did?

Please, God. Let it be so.

Once inside, Lilly slipped her hand from his and removed her cloak, draping it across a nearby armchair.

His breath hitched.

God help him.

She wore that incredible red gown she had bought in the village with him that day. The one that enhanced every one of her luscious curves.

Desire, scorching and untamed, tunneled through Layton's veins, putting the crackling fire in the hearth to shame.

Wait.

A fire?

Lilly only allowed fires in occupied rooms and even then, only small blazes. Barely enough to keep the chill at bay.

He veered a glance toward the door.

As if she had read his mind, she gave him a naughty smile.

"I locked it before coming outside to meet you, Layton."

Had Lilly expected to come in here with him, the little vixen?

"Lilibet Granger?"

He stalked nearer to her, delighted when her eyes rounded, and she licked her lower lip.

"Have you been playing hard-to-get, minx? Did you hope to make me grovel, for I shall? Without hesitation or reserve."

Layton dropped to his knees, then clasped her icy hands.

"Tell me that I have not misplaced my hope, Lilly."

He pressed his mouth to her knuckles.

"You silly man." Emotion made her voice husky. "Of course, you have not. I love you too."

With a whoop, Layton sprang to his feet and swooped her into his arms, capturing her mouth with his. He kissed her with the passion and intensity of a dying man who had been given another chance at life.

For that is exactly what she had done.

Lilly had healed his wounded soul.

Layton lifted his head.

Lips parted, her breath coming in soft little pants, she

raised her thick eyelashes. Passion had darkened her eyes to almost black. "I am still cold."

The tease.

"I think it is time I taught the headmistress a lesson or two." Layton carried her to the settee and gently laid her down before kneeling beside her.

"Something tells me, you are a fast learner, Lilly."

Her seductive smile quickened his pulse into a full-on stampede.

"True." Her smile turned coy. "But especially so if I have an excellent teacher."

Nuzzling her silky neck, he worked the buttons of her gown. "You will marry me?"

If she said no, Layton would have to stop.

It might kill him, but he would, and then dive into the brook to cool his ardor.

"Of course, I shall marry you, dear heart." She made a cute little face. "But I want all the children, Charles, and the staff present at our wedding. Your family too, of course."

She pressed a kiss to his chin and then his cheek and then his eyepatch.

Tears formed in his good eye.

Lilly had never shied away from Layton's disfigurement.

"I would not have it any other way." He finished slipping the buttons loose of their moorings and the gown fell open, revealing the tempting mounds beneath her simple cotton chemise.

"This is like a dream," she murmured huskily. "Am I awake?"

"Indeed, my love." Layton brushed a kiss across her swollen mouth. "You are my dream come true."

"And you are mine." She looped her arms around his neck. "Shall we begin?"

Throwing his head back, Layton laughed, at last free from the ghosts of his past.

EPILOGUE

Hefferwickshire House Chapel
Cumberland, England

September 1832—ten in the morning

From across the baptismal font, Layton caught Lilly's eye as The Reverend Tyndale sprinkled water on their month-old son's forehead. "I baptize thee in the name of the Father, and of the Son, and of the Holy Ghost."

Happier than Layton had ever imagined he could be, his heart swelled with love. How he cherished her and their children.

She swept her mouth upward in an adoring smile before shifting her doting attention to their second child: Xander Caspius Magnus Westbrook.

The reverend passed the sleeping infant back to one of his godfathers.

Fletcher, cradled his godson, crooning softly to the child.

Siobhan, his wife and one of the babe's godmothers,

smoothed a hand across her swollen belly. Soon, another Westbrook would join the ever-growing family.

The other godparents, Charles and his wife Charlene—the former Miss McKenzie—exchanged a meaningful glance. Their child would arrive in the spring.

Charles had finally convinced Charlene that he didn't care if she was older than him. Love does not keep an account of age, he vowed.

They had married last year, much to Lilly's delight.

"Let us bow our heads in prayer." The Rector closed his eyes, and those standing around the baptismal font as well as the Westbrooks sitting in the pews obliged.

"May the peace of God, which passeth all understanding, keep your hearts and minds in the knowledge and love of God, and of his Son Jesus Christ our Lord: and the blessing of God Almighty, the Father, the Son, and the Holy Ghost, be amongst you, and remain with you always. Amen."

"Amen," Layton murmured as the "Amens," of the others filled the quaint chapel, he and Lilly had exchanged vows in almost four years ago.

"Thank you, Reverend Tyndale. I hope you and Mrs. Tyndale can join us at the great house for refreshments." Layton extended his hand, which the man of God clasped at once.

"It would be my pleasure, Captain Westbrook." Smiling, the vicar glanced around the noisy sanctuary. "I believe your little fellow brings the total of Westbrook babe baptisms I have performed in the last few years to eighteen."

The Westbrooks had always been a fertile family.

Layton's adopted father, the Duke of Latham, had five brothers, and between them, they boasted two and thirty children, not counting Father's eight. Father had nine and thirty first cousins. When one included their spouses and offspring, they numbered in the hundreds.

Eyes twinkling, the reverend nodded toward the extended family milling about the pews. "It appears I shall have the pleasure a few more times soon."

"Indeed," Layton replied dryly before the reverend turned to greet the Duke of Latham.

Not only was Siobhan expecting, so were four of Layton's sisters-in-law and his sister, Althelia, as well.

Surrounded by grandchildren, Mother was in her element.

"Mama." Mattie fussed in her grandmother's arms, and the duchess bounced the almost twenty-month-old, trying to soothe her. "Mama."

Lilly swept to her daughter. "Mama is here, darling."

Mattie, named after Matilda Davenport, laid her head on her mother's chest and calmed at once, toying with the triple strand of pearls around Lilly's neck.

Pearls were the only jewels that Lilly wore.

She claimed other gemstones were too flamboyant for her simple country tastes.

Layton had known Lilly would make a magnificent mother. That was why she loved the orphans so much. She was a natural nurturer.

Fletcher appeared at his side, still holding Xander.

Lilly and Layton had not discussed another name for their son, though they did change the spelling. It seemed the perfect name and would always remind them of how they met.

"This little chap is the first Westbrook to sleep through his baptism." Fletcher traced a finger over the baby's soft cheek. "I think he may be a taciturn fellow like his father," he teased, good-naturedly.

"Stow it, brother. Xander is a cheerful, contented babe." The truth was, that until Lilly came into his life, Layton had been an aloof bore.

"Here." Fletcher gently set Xander in Layton's arms. "My wife needs a hand with our energetic offspring."

With so many children under the age of four, family gatherings were chaotic, at best.

"My mother would have adored this."

Father had approached silently and stood just behind Layton.

Layton nodded. "She would have indeed. The first chance she had, she would have sneaked the children treats and regaled them with mystical Roma tales."

Father chuckled. "She was something else."

Grandmama had passed nine months ago, and the family had still not adjusted to the matriarch's absence.

Excusing herself, Lilly left Mother chatting with Cassius and Beatrice. With Mattie in her arms, Lilly met Layton at the front of the chapel.

"Happy, my love?" He kissed their daughter's dark blond head.

"Exquisitely so." Lilly rested her cheek against his shoulder. "If you had told me four years ago that I would be content unless I was headmistress at Kelston Hall's Children's Home, I would have said you were daft. But then I did not think I would ever marry either."

"Your role as administrator for Kelston Hall keeps you plenty busy, my dear."

Though Lilly no longer acted as the home's director or headmistress, she oversaw the operation. No man could have done a finer job either. She often sought Layton's advice, insisting the home was as much his because of the trust fund he had established.

Since their marriage in December of 1828, Lilly had expanded Kelston Hall, even drawing the schematics for the developments herself. The home now housed over one hundred children.

Layton had assisted her in hiring additional staff,

including a new director, headmistress, grounds keeper, and a man of all work.

"This afternoon, I thought we could speak with your parents about the charity ball." She glanced upward, a twinkle in her brown eyes. "I do not think they realized just what they volunteered for, but they have been ever so helpful."

"Have I told you that you never cease to amaze me, darling?" Layton wrapped an arm around her shoulders. "I do not know any other woman who could convince so many aristocrats to open their purse strings to help orphaned children. I believe you have started a movement."

"Well, someone has to help them." Her cheeks glowed pink as she spoke about her passion. "At the very least, they should be provided food, clothing, and a basic education."

"I agree." He lowered his head and brushed a kiss against her ear.

She shivered.

"Behave yourself, Layton," she whispered fiercely. "You know I cannot resist you."

Chuckling wickedly, he lifted her chin. "I know."

He then proceeded to kiss her soundly, only separating when loud applause broke the spell.

"Layton Westbrook, you are a scoundrel," Lilly said breathlessly, but her shining eyes belied any true censure.

He winked. "Oh, I do hope so my love."

THE END

I hope you enjoyed
ONCE UPON A MIDNIGHT DREAM
and following Layton and Lilly's romantic journey.
If you would like to leave a review,
I would be very grateful.

. . .

Keep reading for a free preview of
A YULETIDE TOSS OF THE DICE
Book 1
Ladies of Opportunity Series...

FREE PREVIEW

A YULETIDE TOSS OF THE DICE

Gloucester Street, London

8 December 1818

I'm late again.

Without waiting for the aging driver to climb down, lower the step, and wrench open the outdated coach's door, Aubriella Penford agilely hopped from the conveyance just as it rolled to a stop before the Danforths' unobtrusive townhome in the quasi-fashionable London neighborhood.

The hot coals inside the foot warmer had done little to alleviate the vehicle's chill, yet the frigid air slapping her cheeks upon her descent onto the pavement caused her to inhale sharply. Huddled into her new raspberry-red and black redingote—how Aubriella adored the vibrant shade—she shivered as she waved Mosely back to his seat.

"No need to come down, Mosely."

The sooner she was inside, the sooner he could find himself a cozy table in Ye Olde Cheshire Cheese pub and enjoy a pint or two while flirting with Widow Waddell.

Aubriella darted a swift glance toward the house, unsurprised to see a yellowed lace curtain pushed aside and Roxina Danforth peering at the lane. A wry smile curving her mouth, she fluttered her fingers at Aubriella before permitting the panel to fall into place once more. Likely so that she could tell the others that Aubriella had finally arrived.

Against her will, her attention slid to the equally unremarkable but tidy brick townhouse next door before she jerked it away. The Matherfield brothers lived there. Jackson Matherfield, the eldest and a close friend of her brother's, had been a sharp, irritating pebble in her shoe for the better part of fifteen years.

Aubriella tightened her jaw, vexed at her lack of self-control as much as her continual lack of punctuality.

She loathed making her friends wait, but escaping the house wasn't easy. Mama must be informed and approve of Aubriella's use of the coach. Jessamine, her seventeen-year-old sister, often begged to come along, which simply would not do for the weekly meetings with the *Ladies of Opportunity,* as they jokingly referred to themselves.

The group, a secret society, kept a betting book much like White's, but which was reserved exclusively for female patrons. That criteria prevented women from becoming indebted to male creditors, which might risk their virtue.

Imagine the *haut ton's* shock should the client list or the nature of the numerous wagers ever be revealed. That must *never* happen. Women who supplemented their income via secret gambling stakes could expect tarnished reputations or ruin should they be found out.

Believable excuses must be contrived to dissuade Aubriella's social butterfly of a sister from accompanying her, and one could not easily deter Minnie. In all fairness to her mother and sister, Aubriella often lost track of time while researching and studying, which, more than anything, accounted for her perpetual tardiness.

Shutting the door, she cast a pensive glance at the ominous pewter sky as she approached the coach's front.

It looks like it may snow.

She gave a joyous internal whoop.

Please. Please. Please snow.

Winter had finally arrived, bringing bitter cold and the possibility of a much-desired snowstorm.

None too soon, either.

Now, if only a foot or two of freezing white fluff would fall and remain on the ground, preventing her family from attending the Templetons' annual Christmastide house party in Westerham. A fortnight of holiday revelry, tedious parlor games, gambling, impromptu recitals, awful skits, and dancing, of course.

All of which Aubriella was wholly inept at, except the wagering.

That particular vice she had become very adept at, indeed.

Her sisters had inherited Mama's fair coloring, curves, beauty, gracefulness, and adoration of all things social. Aubriella took after their father: dark, freckled, thin, and, as Papa was wont to say, "amiably awkward."

Kind but clumsy.

Genial but gauche.

His good-natured maladroitness was endearing.

Hers?

Nothing short of humiliating.

What was worse, the Templetons believed in the adage, *the more the merrier*, and packed the house to the rafters with revelers. That, along with too much mulled wine, hot toddies, abundant champagne, and the gentlemen imbibing in stronger spirits, provided the perfect opportunity for illicit liaisons.

Last year, trying to find a quiet spot to read, she'd stumbled upon no fewer than three amorous couples. That included Jackson Matherfield in the conservatory wrapped in a scandalous embrace with that fast, immoral wanton Francine Willoughby.

Even now, the memory caused Aubriella's cheeks to flame with chagrin, and it was freezing outside. She'd pelted back to her shared bedchamber and pleaded a sick headache for the next four and twenty hours.

Never mind that Aubriella didn't ever suffer from headaches.

But what she'd accidentally witnessed made her head throb with the vengeance of a Highlander's battle drums and proved beyond a doubt that Jackson Matherfield was every bit the rapscallion and rakehell she'd always believed him to be.

Mindful that her friends awaited her, Aubriella slung her satchel strap over her head and adjusted the bag to hang near her waist. The smooth, dark-brown leather concealed so many secrets. Confidences she and the others she was about to meet with had sworn never to reveal.

Keeping one hand firmly against the sealed bag, she peered up at Mosely.

"Pick me up in three hours." Would that give her enough time to ready herself for dinner? "No, you had better make it two."

Mama had invited guests to supper for Emmet's birthday, although for the life of her, Aubriella couldn't remember precisely who would attend and celebrate.

Had Mama told her?

Probably.

Trying to recall, Aubriella pursed her lips. Absorbed with the drawings she'd received from Italy last week, not much else had kept her attention these past few days.

Such magnificent, wondrous, intriguing renderings.

The copies of Leonardo da Vinci's anatomical drawings lay hidden beneath her mattress.

Just thinking about the intricate and detailed works caused her tummy to tumble with giddiness. She *might've* led her parents to believe the sketches were da Vinci's architectural renderings. Architecture wasn't exactly appropriate for a young lady of quality, but it was certainly not as scandalous as the artist's depictions of human dissections.

Aubriella felt little remorse for deceiving her parents.

If women could study medicine, she wouldn't have had to resort to subterfuge. However, until that day came—and she was confident it must—she would unapologetically use whatever means necessary to expand her knowledge of the human body.

Regardless, a formal supper meant Aubriella must dress appropriately. Her usual attire of whatever she wore while studying her specimens would not do, sans her stained laboratory apron, of course.

No, tonight would require a fashionable gown, stays, intricately coiffured hair, jewelry, and perfume. And, of course, her best manners, decorum, and *hours* of insipid small talk. She would struggle to not roll her eyes, yawn, or make a less-than-charitable remark.

So help her God, if anyone mentioned the weather, fashion, or shared a snippet of gossip, she would eschew propriety and suggest a dark, unmentionable cavern where they might shove said exchange.

Since at four and twenty, she was too old to banish to her room, and restricting her social interactions merely brought her relief, her parents had no notion what to do with their middle daughter when she blurted something blush-worthy or indecorous. Which, truth be told, occurred more often than Aubriella cared to admit.

Nevertheless, the skills that came easily to her sisters

seemed to have skipped her altogether, along with the ability to dance gracefully, sing in tune, and wield a needle with any skill. Although she'd bet her pin money if women could become surgeons, she'd have managed a needle with considerable aptitude.

Yes, tonight would be another painful reminder of everything Aubriella was and was not. She was plain, solidly on the shelf, and had nothing to look forward to except caring for her parents in their dotage.

And...sneaking around, trying to learn as much about anatomy as possible.

A sparrow amongst doves.

For certain, tonight she would say something stupid, knock over her wineglass, clink her fork or spoon against her plate, or any number of other miniature calamities.

One could wager on it.

Her stomach cramped at the thought, but she forced a smile to her suddenly stiff lips.

"Please tell Widow Waddell hello for me, Mosely."

For the past year, since entering into the clandestine *business venture*, she'd visited Roxina almost weekly. Mosely and the widow had grown quite cozy, and Aubriella hoped he'd propose soon.

"Yes, Miss Penford. I shall." He nodded, giving her a grateful smile, fondness creasing the corners of his kind, nut-brown eyes and wrinkling his weathered face. "I'll just watch until you've entered the house."

He took his duties to deliver Aubriella home unharmed seriously. That meant he was on duty until the door closed behind her. Bracing against the wintry wind buffeting her, she bent her head as she turned and plowed straight into a tall, hard, masculine form.

"Careful there, Miss Penford."

FROM THE DESK OF
COLLETTE CAMERON®

Thank you for reading ONCE UPON A MIDNIGHT DREAM. As always, I am sad when a series ends but also excited to move on to the next books romping around in my head.

From the time I introduced Layton Westbrook in MIDNIGHT CHRISTMAS WALTZ, I wanted him to have a large family. In fact, I made a note to myself to have him meet his sweetheart at a foundling home. Nine stories later, a woman who lives near Prudhoe, England and oversees an orphanage rescues him. My muse never fails me.

Historical accuracy is important to me, and to the extent I am able, though my stories are fictional, I strive to ensure details I include could have taken place. Since Lilly and Mrs. Davenport had pox scars, there needed to be at least one small pox outbreak to make the story believable. Through my research, I discovered that there was a major outbreak in London in 1770, but that the disease was endemic, meaning it was constantly present in the population and outbreaks would flare up periodically.

I want to clarify a couple of factual tidbits, in case any of my readers are historical sleuths. There is a brook called Hodgson Burn that flows through part of the countryside around Prudhoe. I took artistic liberty and used the brook for the story, even though Kelston Hall's exact location is fictional.

Smuggling was a common enterprise around Berwick-upon-Tweed. I am always delighted when an idea pops into my mind while I am writing, and after a bit of research, I discover my notion is verified.

Though I have written over sixty-five books, I learned something new while researching for this story. I have used the terms *le beau monde* and *haut ton* many, many times regarding High Society in my romances. What I did not know was that each was also a fashionable periodical. *Le Beau Monde* was also known as *Literary and Fashionable Magazine*, while *Haut Ton* was also known as *High Life in London*.

Guy Fawkes Night celebrations were well established in England by 1828. The fireworks and "sparklers" of that day posed a significant risk, and although children ran about carrying firebrands, I opted not to have the orphans do so.

While it is reasonable to assume fireworks displays may have taken place in or near Prudhoe, the scale and visibility of the celebrations are not noted historically. The fireworks would have been mostly yellow, orange, and white or silver. Other colors had not been widely developed yet.

Mocha coffee came from the Yemini highlands, and although it had a slightly chocolatey taste, that is not how the coffee acquired its name. The term Mocha coffee originates from the port city of Mocha (Al Mokha) in Yemin, which was a significant coffee trade center.

One last note... Slavery was still very much in place in 1828 Morocco. European Christians were captured through piracy and raids. Those not held for ransom were kept as servants.

I hope you enjoyed a few hours' escape while reading Layton and Lilly's story.

Hugs,
Collette Cameron®

If you haven't joined Collette's exclusive mailing list click on QR image to sign up! You'll get access to exclusive content, sneak peeks, contests, giveaways, and more...

(P.S. No spam!)

https://bit.ly/TheRegencyRoseGift

**Collette loves to hear from readers.
You can contact her via her website:
collettecameron.com.
Or email her directly at collette@collettecameron-books.com.**

**You can also follow Collette on social media:
Facebook:** https://www.facebook.com/
CollletteCameronNovels/
Instagram: https://instagram.com/collettecameronauthor/
Goodreads: https://www.goodreads.com/collettecameron
Book Bub: https://www.bookbub.com/authors/collette-cameron

Pinterest: http://www.pinterest.com/colletteauthor/
YouTube: https://www.youtube.com/@
ColletteCameronAuthor

Giggles are Guaranteed
Collette's Cheris Reader Group

https://www.facebook.com/groups/CollettesCheris/

If you love to chat about all things romance-book related and enjoy taking part in fun and engaging live events, contests, and giveaways join **Collette's Chèris VIP Reader Group, https://www.facebook.com/groups/CollettesCheris/,** my exclusive private book group on Facebook.

Giggles are guaranteed!

Hope to see you there,
Collette Cameron®

ABOUT THE AUTHOR

COLLETTE CAMERON®

USA Today Bestselling author Collette Cameron® is renowned for her captivating, humorous, and heartwarming Scottish and Regency historical romance novels. With over 65 published titles, over 1.6 million books sold around the world, and multiple writing awards to her credit, Collette is a well-known author in the world of historical romance.

Readers love her witty and relatable characters including daring rogues, dashing scoundrels, and the strong and spirited heroines who capture their hearts. From the rugged highlands to the refined drawing rooms of Regency England, Collette's novels will transport you to another time and place, where love and adventure are just a page away.

Collette's Sweet-to-Spicy Timeless Romances® are the perfect escape for readers looking for romantic escape, poignant inspiration, engaging humor, and entertaining stories.

Based in the Pacific Northwest, Collette is surrounded by the lush greenery and rainy skies that inspire her writing. She dreams of one day splitting her time between the Pacific Northwest and Scotland. In the meantime, she indulges in her love of all things cobalt blue, dachshunds, chocolate, and of course, crafting her next historical romance.

Blue Rose Romance® LLC
collette@collettecameronbooks.com
collettecameron.com

ALSO BY COLLETTE CAMERON®

BLUE ROSE ROMANCE® LLC
COLLETTE CAMERON'S® COMPLETE BOOK LIST

CHRONICLES OF THE WESTBROOK BRIDES
A Romantic Opposites Attract Mystery & Suspense
Family Saga Regency Romance

Midnight Christmas Waltz — Book 1

Mission at Midnight — Book 2

The Midnight Marquess — Book 3

Holly, Mistletoe, and Midnight Snow — Book 4

The Wallflower's Midnight Waltz— Book 5

Minuet at Midnight— Book 6

Kiss a Rake at Midnight — Book 7

Unmasked at Midnight — Book 8

Memories Made at Midnight — Book 9

Once Upon a Midnight Dream — Book 10

LADIES OF OPPORTUNITY

A Bluestockings and Rogues Opposites Attract
Regency Mystery Christmas Romance

A Yuletide Toss of the Dice — Book 1

SEDUCTIVE SCOUNDRELS

A Sensual Marriage of Convenience

Regency Historical Romance

A Diamond for a Duke — Book 1

Only a Duke Would Dare — Book 2

A December with a Duke — Book 3

What Would a Duke Do? — Book 4

Wooed by a Wicked Duke — Book 5

Duchess of His Heart — Book 6

Never Dance with a Duke — Book 7

Wedding Her Christmas Duke — Book 8

The Debutante and the Duke — Book 9

Loved by a Dangerous Duke — Book 10

How to Win a Duke's Heart — Book 11

When a Duke Desires a Lass — Book 12

My Dearest Duke — Book 13

FOR THE LOVE OF AN EARL (Wicked Earls' Club)

A Humorous Aristocrat and Wallflower

Regency Romance Adventure

Earl of Wainthorpe — Book 1

Earl of Scarborough — Book 2

Earl of Keyworth — Book 3

Earl of Renshaw — Book 4

HEART OF A SCOT

A Passionate Enemies to Lovers

Scottish Highlander Historical Mystery

Romance Adventure

To Love a Highland Laird — Book 1

To Redeem a Highland Rogue — Book 2

To Seduce a Highland Scoundrel — Book 3

To Woo a Highland Warrior — Book 4

To Enchant a Highland Earl — Book 5

To Defy a Highland Duke — Book 6

To Marry a Highland Marauder — Book 7

To Bargain with a Highland Buccaneer — Book 8

A Christmas Kiss for the Highlander — Book 9

HIGHLAND HEATHER ROMANCING A SCOT: CASTLE BRIDES

A Passionate Enemies to Lovers Second Chance

Scottish Highlander Mystery Romance

Heart of a Highlander — Prequel

The Viscount's Vow — Book 1

The Highlander's Heiress — Book 2

The Earl's Enticement — Book 3

Triumph and Treasure — Book 4

Virtue and Valor — Book 5

Heartbreak and Honor — Book

Scandal's Splendor — Book 7

Passion and Plunder — Book 8

Wishes and Wonder — Book 9

A Yuletide Highlander — Book 10

DAUGHTERS OF DESIRE (SCANDALOUS LADIES)
A Romantic Class Difference Forced Proximity
Regency Romance with Aristocrats

A Lady, A Wish, A Christmas Wish — Book 1

No Lady for the Lord — Book 2

Love Lessons for a Lady — Book 3

His One and Only Lady — Book 4

Never a Proper Lady — Book 5

Lady Tempts a Rogue — Book 6

THE CULPEPPER MISSES
A Humorous Wallflower Family Saga
Regency Romantic Comedy

The Earl and the Spinster — Book 1
The Marquis and the Vixen — Book 2
The Lord and the Wallflower — Book 3
The Buccaneer and the Bluestocking — Book 4
The Lieutenant and the Lady — Book 5

THE HONORABLE ROGUES®
A Second Chance Redeemable Rogue
and Wallflower Regency Romance

A Kiss for a Rogue — Book 1
A Bride for a Rogue — Book 2
A Rogue's Scandalous Wish — Book 3
To Capture a Rogue's Heart — Book 4
The Rogue and the Wallflower — Book 5
A Rose for a Rogue — Book 6
'Twas the Rogue Before Christmas — Book 7
A Rogue Worth the Risk — Book 8